Night Ambush!

The raiders' fire ripped into the four
blanket-wrapped figures on the ground,
which jerked silently as the bullets
hammered through them. There was a long
moment of suspense—then four men
crept close to the "corpses"—the
dummies Slade had used to bait his trap.

The Ranger stepped forward and
shouted, *"Elevate! You're covered!"*

The raiders moved uncertainly—but Slade's
eyes caught a flash from an unholstered
gun—and both his Colts let go with a
crash. His men joined in, and the raiders
went down like puppets . . .

. . . then from the woods beyond came
an answering bellow of gunfire as
the main group of outlaws rained lead on
the Ranger's party—the trap had been
sprung, and *they* were in it!

BULLETS FOR
A RANGER

BRADFORD · SCOTT

PYRAMID BOOKS • NEW YORK

1

A STORM WAS BLOWING in from Matagorda Bay, driving the gray waters of the Gulf before it in an endless procession of tossing, foam-capped waves. Overhead the cloud wrack writhed and tumbled. From time to time a wild white moon looked down through the rifts, glinted on the wave crests and touched the raving waters with silver fire. Birds scudded down the long slant of the sky like whirling leaves, seeking sanctuary. A great saddle-backed gull breasted the gale with steel-thewed pinions. A very master of the storm, he, harnessing the tempest to his own dark ends.

Twigs and leaves spun through the tortured air. Dead branches showered down from the chaparral. A tree fell with a crash. The wind howled in triumph and whooped across the sands of the beach, swirling the lighter particles in blinding clouds. It was a wild night already, in the last gasp of twilight, and held every promise of becoming even wilder as the hours passed.

Close to the water's edge, where the arc of the bay swept around in a splendid curve, ran a trail. At the very apex of the curve stood a single dead tree, its naked branches swaying with a dry rattle. On one thick limb perched three dilapidated-looking crows sheltered from the blast of the wind by the ponderous trunk. With ruffled feathers, gleaming red eyes and drooping beaks, they appeared in a very bad temper indeed.

Riding north on the trail was a tall and broad-shouldered man on a correspondingly tall black horse. As they neared the dead tree, a terrific gust howled in from the bay. There was a crackling, splitting sound, a rending crash and a resounding thud as the tree gave up the battle of a century with the wind and fell across the trail. The crows, their shelter gone, went away from there with wrathful squawks. One hurtling black projectile, screeching curses, whizzed by so close that it fairly grazed the black horse's nose.

The horse screamed angrily and snapped his milk-white

teeth. Ranger Walt Slade, whom the Mexican *peones* of the Rio Grande river villages named *El Halcón*—The Hawk—rocked in the hull with laughter.

"Take it easy, Shadow," he chided his mount. "That fellow wasn't after you; he was just trying to get in the clear. Lucky for us though, we weren't a few yards farther on. If one of those branches had larruped us, we would have felt it."

The wrathful crow hurtled on, the wind buffeting him, his black feathers glinting in the moonlight that poured through a ragged rift in the cloud wrack. Straight for the shelter of a thicket some three hundred yards farther along the trail he scudded, his two companions screeching along behind him.

But when he reached the thicket, the crow's reaction was peculiar. Suddenly he braked with his wings, rocking backward on the axis of the spread pinions. The wind caught him, and he turned a complete somersault in the air. By a seeming miracle of agility he caught his balance, veered and went streaking away at an angle from the thicket. An instant later he and his speeding companions vanished into a second thicket several hundred yards farther on.

Walt Slade stared after the vanished crows, his black brows drawing together.

"Now what do you suppose set those jiggers off that way?" he asked Shadow. "Looks like they ran smack into something they didn't like the looks of. Must be something holed up in that brush. But what? Takes considerable to scare off crows, and on a night like this a bird will take most any kind of a chance to get under cover. Such a wind is liable to smash him all to pieces against a limb or a tree trunk. But those black galoots took right back against the wind."

He glanced at the sky. "Going to cloud up that moon again in a few minutes," he added. "Reckon we won't take any chances; funny things been happening in this section of late, from all reports."

While the moonlight still streamed down, he veered the horse carefully around the welter of smashed branches blocking the trail. Just before the cloud wrack thickened, he regained the track and rode unconcernedly along it.

But the instant the funnel of moonlight pouring through the rift snapped off like a searchlight beam, he swerved Shadow from the trail and rode due north across the sands to where a straggle of brush that encroached the beach began. The roar of the wind and the groaning of the trees effectually drowned the muffled beat of the horse's irons on the sand.

Walt Slade was trailing ghosts—rather a unique pastime for

a Texas Ranger. But that, in the opinion of many of the section, was what it amounted to. And it was to do just that that Captain Jim McNelty, the famous Commander of the Border Battalion, had sent him to the Matagorda Bay country.

"Men of steel!" snorted Captain Jim. "The old Spaniards in armor come back to life! Just a bunch of brush-poppin' owlhoots, that's what. Sheriff writes asking for a troop of Rangers to get things under control. A troop to chase ghosts! Yes, just a bunch of owlhoots playing on ignorance and superstition. Skalleyhoot down there, Walt, and run 'em into the bay. If you see a real ghost and get scared, send word back and I'll come down myself. Get goin'!"

Slade chuckled at the thought of Captain Jim's tirade, but he did not underestimate the seriousness of the situation. Ignorance and superstition are made to order for the unscrupulous and crafty who know how to make the most of those attributes. Ordinary wide-loopers in wet slickers and dripping "J.B.'s—" that was doubtless the answer. But sheep and cattle had been stolen and men murdered, which required a different "answer."

For several hundred yards Slade rode north; then he veered to the east. Another hundred yards and he pulled Shadow to a halt in the shelter of a clump of chaparral and dismounted.

"You take it easy here for a spell," he told the horse. "I figure that thicket can stand a mite of investigating, and from here on I'll do better on foot. If there is somebody holed up there for some reason or other, doubtless an off-color one, they'd be sure to hear you clumping along. Stay put, and keep quiet."

Confident that Shadow would do both, he stole forward to the edge of the thicket farthest from the trail, slowing to a crawl as he neared the first fringe of growth. It was a ticklish business, that slow stalk through the gloom, with always the threat of the moonlight pouring down again to reveal him to any chance watcher. He figured that anybody concealed in the growth would be keeping an eye on the trail, but of that he couldn't be certain. With a sigh of relief he reached the bristle of chaparral and slid into it. Slowly, cautiously, he glided forward, testing the ground ahead at each step, noiselessly moving branches aside. Objects were eerie and unreal in the faint light that seeped through the cloud bank. As he penetrated deeper into the growth, the dark became absolute. Another score of yards, however, and the brush began to thin. Slade knew he must be close to where the tangle of branches edged the trail. He doubled his caution, straining his ears to catch any sound rising above the turmoil of the storm, peering with narrowed eyes to note the slightest movement amid the shadows. His instinct, developed over years of training, told him that no great distance away there was life, doubtlessly malevolent life. He halted, every sense at hair-trigger alert.

For some time he stood perfectly still, hearing nothing, seeing nothing. Finally he took another cautious step forward, planting his reaching foot on what appeared to be firm earth but was in reality the hard crusted rim of a badger hole. The rim crumbled under his weight and he lurched forward, completely off balance. Instinctively he clutched for support, gripped a welter of dry branches and saved himself from falling; but the branches broke in his grasp with a prodigious snapping and crackling. And at that moment the treacherous cloud wrack curled up like torn paper, letting through a flood of silvery moonlight. The whole scene became bright as day.

Walt Slade saw, facing him, the moonlight shining on the startled forms of two men apparently clad in medieval armor. The moonlight glinted on what looked like plates of steel protecting their chests. It shone on burnished round headpieces that also seemed to be of steel. But it also glinted on the barrels of anything but medieval forty-fives. The barrels jerked up as Slade went for his guns. The air rocked and quivered to the reports. Even in that hectic moment Slade was astounded by what sounded like a clang of metal striking metal.

Through the streams of orange fire and the fog of smoke gushing toward him, Slade saw one of the "men of steel" slew sideways and crash into a tangle of growth. He felt the wind of a passing bullet, heard the screech of another, which nicked his ear. Then two guns roared as one. Slade saw the dry-gulcher hurtle back, steady himself, fire again as the Ranger pulled trigger. A choking cry came from the dry-gulcher as he went down.

But Walt Slade neither saw the fall nor heard the death cry. For at that instant the world about him exploded in scorching flame and blazing light through which rushed a cloud of utter blackness to wrap him fold on clammy fold. Three motionless forms lay amid the brush as the clouds thickened and blotted out the scene of death.

2

><===>

WHEN HE FINALLY regained something resembling consciousness, Slade knew he must have been completely out for some time. His face was caked with dried blood which had flowed from a bullet gash at the hairline above his left temple; his clothes were soaked by rain that had fallen. His limbs were stiff and he was cold. Fortunately, however, the night was warm, and a bit of movement would quickly remedy that condition. There seemed to be a great hammer beating with clanging strokes in his head. Waves of pain flowed before his eyes as he moved, and for a long moment he was deathly sick.

Recovering somewhat, he propped himself on a shaking elbow. Overhead the sky was almost clear, although the wind still howled in intermittent gusts. Summoning his strength, he lurched to his feet to stand weaving and staggering. The effort reopened the wound, and blood trickled down his face. He wiped it away with a trembling hand and glared wildly about.

Nowhere nearby was there any sign of movement. The tossing waves of the bay were silvered by the moonlight, and far out on the turbulent water showed a crawling gleam of light, evidently from a ship breasting the waves.

"And she'd better stay out there," he muttered, apropos of the passing vessel. "Get too close and some contrary current is liable to beach her, and she'd be pounded to pieces in no time."

Dismissing the ship, which could doubtless take care of itself, from his thoughts, he turned his attention to his more immediate surroundings. Shadowy amid the broken growth straggling the sand, he could just make out the sprawled bodies of the two dry-gulchers. He was anxious to examine them, but they'd have to wait.

With fingers that still trembled, he explored the bullet crease. He was reassured in finding no evidence of fracture, a conclusion bolstered by the free flow of blood. Concussion might be another matter, but he did not think he had suffered any. Just the same, the blasted thing must be taken care of, and without delay.

Stumbling and lurching, he made his way to where Shadow was waiting in patient disgust. He fumbled a jar of antiseptic ointment and a roll of bandage from his saddle pouch. After smearing the wound with the ointment, he padded it heavily and managed to bandage the pad into place. The activity warmed him, and he decided he was feeling a mite better despite the hammer blows inside his head, which were lessening to a degree.

"Okay, feller, now for you," he told the horse, and proceeded to loosen the cinches and flip the bit free so that the animal could graze in comfort on the sparse grass, which Shadow immediately proceeded to do. The task completed, Slade turned to search out a resting spot for himself. As he did so, his attention was attracted by a glow in the northeast, miles distant, steadily brightening against the sky. It quickly resolved to a flicker of flame tossing and billowing in the wind. He knew it was a beacon atop a hill to notify the coming ship that it was safe to veer nearer the land into a channel that would lead it to port.

Still feeling far from good, Slade sat down with his back against a tree trunk, fished out his waterproof pouch of tobacco and papers and rolled a cigarette, his hands still shaking slightly. The blasted slug had hit him one devil of a wallop.

"Guess I'm lucky at that, though," he told Shadow. "Another inch to the right and I wouldn't be here talking to you about it."

He smoked the cigarette slowly, down to a short butt, which he pinched out and cast aside. Feeling somewhat better, he got to his feet.

"Now for a look at those gents in 'armor,'" he said. He was very curious about the bizarre costume the pair affected and wanted to know just what it was that bore such a remarkable resemblance to what the iron men of Spain wore some centuries ago. He strode to the edge of the growth, from where he could see the bodies sprawled on the sand. Pausing, he glanced around, started forward again and halted in mid-stride.

To the east the moonlit trail was visible for nearly a mile. Riding the trail and steadily drawing nearer the thicket were seven or eight horsemen. As they approached, Slade saw that the moonlight reflected from burnished headpieces and whatever the devil it was that covered their breasts.

"More of the same brand!" he growled, eyeing the approaching riders.

Just what would be best to do, he wondered. Quite likely they were coming to look for the two who had holed up in the thicket. They wouldn't have any trouble spotting the bodies from the trail. But would they perhaps search the growth for a clue as to what had happened to them? That was a very serious question from the Ranger's point of view. He was in no shape to take on odds of eight to one. And he certainly didn't feel like being the quarry in a grueling chase. He had every faith in Shadow's speed and endurance, but even the best of horses needs a guiding hand that is sure, and at the moment his hand was far from sure. The sensible thing was to stay holed up in the growth and hope for the best. He moved back a little to where he could see but not be seen, and waited.

The approaching horsemen were looming large now, and as the wind lulled for a moment, Slade could hear the click of the speeding irons. A moment later, as they drew abreast of the thicket, an angry shout sounded and another. A gust of oaths followed as there was no answer to the hail. The horses clattered to a halt; several of the riders dismounted. Slade waited. There came a yelp of discovery, then a torrent of curses. The others dismounted hurriedly, and the whole bunch grouped around the two bodies. Strident voices bawled incoherent questions liberally sprinkled with appalling profanity. Slade's hands dropped to his gun butts as several turned toward the thicket.

However, they did not move in his direction. Instead, they hurried toward the far end of the thicket, to the east. A moment later there was another shout of discovery. Two saddled and bridled horses were led into view. The babble of voices rose to an incoherent uproar.

"Dead! Drilled dead center!"

"Who did it? What happened?"

"Who the blankety-blank-blank knows who did it or what happened! They're dead, ain't they? Been dead quite a while, too! No wonder there wasn't any blaze!"

"What a night this has been! A nice haul gone to the blankety-blank-blank!"

"Shut up! Rope 'em to the saddles and let's get out of here. I don't like this business."

Such were the solid peaks above the clouds of indecipherable bumbling. A few minutes later the band mounted and stormed west, the two bodies flopping grotesquely across the saddles of the lead horses, their "armor" reflecting derisive gleams of moonlight.

Little less bewildered than the mysterious night riders, Walt Slade gazed after them until they dwindled from sight. He shook his aching head and returned to Shadow. The whole blasted affair just didn't make sense. Well, he was in no shape to try to think things out. And he had a twenty-mile ride ahead of him.

Not tonight! He doubted if he could stay in the hull for half that distance. So he got the rig off Shadow and gave him a rubdown, after a fashion. His blanket, rolled inside his slicker, was dry. He spread it on the ground, and with his damp saddle for a pillow was almost instantly asleep.

With the full light of dawn he was awake. Aside from a sore head and a sense of frustration, he was about his normal self again. Also he was hungry, a good sign. That could be taken care of. From his saddle pouches he drew forth a slab of bacon, a hunch of bread, some eggs carefully wrapped against breakage, and coffee, along with a small skillet and a little flat bucket. He recalled that only a couple of hundred yards west of his misadventure with the crows there was a trickle of water running down to the bay. So, very soon coffee was bubbling in the bucket, bacon and eggs sizzling in the skillet—all a man needed to banish the pangs of hunger.

After eating and cleaning up, he enjoyed a leisurely smoke, then took stock of his surroundings.

The thicket grew on the crest of a rise that was in the nature of a broad sand dune, the waters of the bay, now blue and placid, washing the base of its gentle slope some seventy feet lower down. There appeared to be nothing outstanding about the spot except that it afforded a good view for some distance across the bay, also along the trail to the east where it began to curve northward, following the contours of the bay.

He walked east to where the horses of the two night riders had been tethered. Here he discovered a big heap of twigs and dry branches. Looked like the band had planned to light a fire and cook a meal, the chore being assigned to the pair holed up in the thicket.

But why at such an isolated spot exposed to the full fury of the wind? The whole business just didn't seem to make sense. Of course, there were sheep and cattle ranches farther west, and it seemed that wide-looping of both cows and woollies had been plaguing the section. And a mile or so to the west was a sheltered cove where a small vessel could put in safely when the weather was not too bad. Would have been risky last night, however.

Slade knew that many of the little coastwise ships that plied the bay and often put in at Port Lavaca were not above handling contraband and doing a bit of genteel smuggling on the side. There was nothing new about running wide-looped cows by water, and sheep would be even easier to handle that way. Perhaps that was the answer to the puzzle. He recalled one of the voices mentioning something about a blaze that wasn't lit. Yes, quite likely that was the explanation. The bunch aimed to eat and hole up here until a bit later, then swoop down on some outlying flock or herd and run a few head to the water's edge, where they would have been taken aboard by a vessel putting in at a given signal. But they picked one devil of a night to try it.

Well, he had been sent here to run down a few ghosts. Anyhow, he'd made a start, at the expense of a sore head. Two of the devils accounted for. Not so bad for his first twenty-four hours in the section. In a more cheerful frame of mind he got the rig on Shadow and headed for Port Lavaca and a bluff on the west shore of Lavaca Bay, an offshoot of Matagorda.

Where the trail curved to the north, he pulled up a moment and sat gazing at the bay. Here the coast was really bad, studded with jagged rocks, the water swirling and eddying over sunken reefs, currents that for seemingly unexplainable reasons ran in madly from the deep water far out. For several miles it would continue thus, to be replaced gradually by a deep and smooth channel along which a ship could sail safely to Port Lavaca. Where the channel began, the beacon had been lighted the night before, to guide the incoming vessel, warning it to stand well out to sea until the treacherous stretch of coast was passed.

Those currents interested Slade, indicating as they did a peculiar geological formation of some sort.

Shortly before the death of his father, subsequent to financial reversals that entailed the loss of the elder Slade's ranch, young Walt had graduated from a famous school of engineering. He had planned to take a post-graduate course in special subjects to round out his education and better fit himself for the profession he determined to make his life's work. This for the time being became impossible, and Slade was at loose ends, undecided as to just what he should do.

Captain Jim McNelty, understanding his predicament, made a suggestion.

"Why not come into the Rangers for a while, Walt," he said. "You will have plenty of spare time to study. You did all right when you were working with me during summer vacations, and we can use you. What do you say?"

Thinking the matter over, Slade decided the suggestion was a good one. Which it turned out to be. Long since he had gotten more from private study than he could have hoped for from the post-grad, and he was eminently fitted to take up the profession of engineering.

But meanwhile Ranger work had gotten a strong hold on him, and he was reluctant to sever connections with the illustrious body of peace officers. Captain Jim smiled when Slade mentioned the fact, but he held his peace, allowing Walt to make up his own mind.

The final result of considerable soul-searching was Slade's decision to stick with the Rangers for a while. He was young—plenty of time to become an engineer. Captain Jim smiled again and refrained from comment. He'd made a similar decision himself, long years ago.

Often Slade had found his knowledge of the principles of engineering of value in the course of his Ranger activities and had put it to use. So now he surveyed the turbulent water with the eye of a geologist.

Two currents interested him particularly. One—broad, turbulent, evidently deep—came storming in from the bay. It headed straight for the face of the beetling, clifflike rocks. The other, not far to the west, flowing outward, was much more placid despite the buffeting of the incoming tide.

"Tide's at flood and this one here is just boiling in, but it doesn't seem to smash the rocks with the force that would be expected," he remarked to Shadow, musingly. "Interesting. Well, june along, horse, we've got things other than speculation over the vagaries of ocean currents to bother about. Let's go!"

To the west and north was rangeland, on which herds of cows grazed. This section, not so long before, Slade knew, was part of Shanghai Pierce's great holdings. Shadow splashed through several shallow bayous. To the west, Slade noted a number of rises, none of them very high, but rugged, with here and there spires of stone.

"Yes, an interesting section, geologically speaking," he told Shadow. "Much weathered down. In the old days, ages before, when the shore of the bay was farther east, it must have been high and rocky. I've a notion that underneath the soil is still the original sedimentary limestone formation, no doubt honeycombed with caves and tunnels which once had openings above ground. Largely conjecture, however, horse, so we won't bother our heads about it. No concern of ours, anyhow."

Shadow snorted agreement, as much as to say, "Okay! Okay! But how about a helpin' of oats before long? I'm more interested in that than limestone caves; oats don't grow in caves."

At least that was Slade's translation of the initial snort, which was followed by a couple more. Who can say he was wrong?

3

IT WAS WELL PAST NOON when El Halcón rode into Port Lavaca, which reeked with the smell of fish and the unsavory aroma of packing houses.

Slade was familiar with the bay town's colorful history, the present town being on the approximate site of Linnville, which was destroyed by enraged Comanches. Burning with anger over the slaughter of their leaders in the Council House fight in San Antonio, an army of five hundred Indians had laid waste to Victoria and marched on Linnville. The residents, believing them to be Mexican traders, took no precautions until it was too late. But before the town was completely surrounded, they realized what was up and took refuge in a big lighter out on the bay beyond arrow shot. The Indians stole everything they could pack away and burned what they couldn't, loaded their loot on fifteen hundred captured horses and departed. Later on, Port Lavaca, "Port of the Cow," rose on the ruins of Linnville.

The town was still a rather important place of entry, but the currents and tides of Matagorda Bay were already slowly choking the channel with silt and destroying the deep water facilities. Port Lavaca would know an era of stagnation until the development of oil and exploitation of recreation facilities would cause it to boom again.

However, it was still plenty lively and still making history when Walt Slade rode in late that beautiful afternoon.

After locating a suitable stable for his horse and making sure all his needs were provided for, Slade headed for the sheriff's office, hoping that official would be in.

Sheriff Neale Ross was in, dozing comfortably in an armchair, his feet propped on his desk. Looked like he didn't have a care in the world, but in fact he had plenty.

The sheriff slowly opened one eye as Slade entered. Then the other snapped open, and his boots hit the floor with a thud.

"Slade!" he shouted. "Where in tarnation did you come from?"

"Over west," Slade replied, grinning at the sheriff's astonishment.

Ross surged to his feet and held out a big paw. They shook solemnly.

"Have a chair," he said. "Make yourself comfortable. Hey, what's the matter? Your head's tied up."

"Leaned against the hot end of a passing slug," Slade answered cheerfully. "Just a scratch."

The sheriff shook his own red head resignedly.

"All right, where are the bodies," he sighed. "I'll go pack 'em in."

"I wish I knew," Slade said.

"Now what the devil do you mean by that?" demanded Ross.

"Sit down, Neale, and I'll tell you about it," Slade replied, and proceeded to do so.

The sheriff swore whole-heartedly as the tale progressed. "The men of steel, eh?" he growled. "And you actually saw them?"

"Yes, I saw them," Slade admitted. "Were wearing what looked like armor, all right, but it wasn't very good armor —didn't offer much protection against a .45. But the lead they threw at me certainly wasn't medieval—it was plumb up to date. I wish I had gotten a close look at what they were wearing, but for a while I wasn't in much shape to do any looking, and when the rest of the bunch showed up, I figured odds of eight to one were a bit lopsided, even if I had been up to snuff, which I certainly was not."

"So I imagine," nodded the sheriff. Suddenly he grinned.

"So!" he chuckled. "I write to McNelty asking for a troop to restore order and he sends me El Halcón, the notorious owlhoot. Oh, well, guess it might be worse. Just suppose there were two El Halcóns. That would be a real calamity, the way trouble always shows up when there's just one of you around. And I've got enough as it is."

"Neale, what *is* going on here?" Slade asked. The sheriff proceeded to enlighten him to the best of his ability.

Like Slade the night before, Sheriff Ross had for some time been trailing "ghosts." At least according to quite a few folks—Ross himself did not think so. He considered it strange and contrary to experience for ghosts to throw hot lead and steal sheep and cows. Which was just what they had been doing, as he wrote Captain McNelty.

In the section there were many sheep ranches, owned chiefly by Texas citizens of Mexican descent or other citizens of out-and-out Indian blood. Embodied in the beliefs of these folks were legends and traditions dealing with the armor-clad men of Spain who had once conquered and overrun the country. As is customary with legendary figures, the men of steel were endowed with awesome and mystical attributes. Strange tales were told beside lonely campfires of the things they did. And the story went on and became a prophecy believed in by many, that, though long vanished from the scene, they would come again in due time and once again rule the land. The simple herders and *peones* of the region believed the stories. So did some not so simple Texas cowhands who should have known better.

Cattle are not the only things in the West that are widelooped. Sheep are worth money, also. They are easy to handle, much easier indeed than obstreperous longhorns; and there are markets for woollies, to those who know where to look for them.

So Sheriff Ross was not particularly surprised when a report came to him that the herders of the section were losing sheep. But he was surprised when more and more reports came in. What was worse, several flock owners had been killed while endeavoring to protect their woollies. Sheriff Ross swore in some special deputies and did his best to run down the wide-loopers. Without success. He found that he was up against a stone wall of fear and superstition on the part of the people he was trying to protect.

He swore in wrathful disgust at the whispers running through the section that the men of steel were once again riding the wastelands. Weird stories were told of men in shining cuirasses and helmets riding through the filtered moonlight of a stormy sky—men it was death to meet, who snatched up herds of sheep and cattle and swept them away into the clouds, never to be seen again.

But the bodies the ghostly riders left behind were plain to be seen, and were found to be punctured by very prosaic and matter-of-fact bullet holes.

Would ghosts use powder and lead to do their killing, he demanded. All too often he was met by an eloquent shoulder shrug and a muttered *quién sabe?* Who knows?

But where do the sheep go, he was asked. And the cows that have been lifted, too. Not to the north, that is certain. Not across seventy miles of desert to the Rio Grande. An expressive glance to the clouds overhead. Profanity from the sheriff.

However, the sheriff figured he had the answer to the

question. Sheep can be transported via ship, and so can cattle. A ship stands in at night. The critters are loaded and away they go to Mexico, or some place else where somebody is waiting to buy them.

"No ships have been seen." To that one the sheriff did *not* have the answer. He was forced to admit that, so far as he knew, it was true.

What irritated Ross most was his inability to obtain reliable information. The herders wouldn't talk. They were brave, hardy men who feared no purely physical dangers. But they shook with terror at the shadows in their own minds. To them the ghostly riders were real and were not of honest flesh and blood.

Finally, in despair, Sheriff Ross wrote to Captain McNelty asking for help. The result: El Halcón, who did not believe in ghosts and in whom the Mexican *peones* and *pastores did* believe.

"So that's how the situation stands," Ross concluded. "I can't learn anything I can depend on, and I can't find out for sure where the blasted critters go. I've had men posted at all the likely coves and inlets; no ship ever shows up. A couple have been spotted standing well out to sea, down south of where the channel begins. If they'd tried it down there, they'd have smashed to the devil against the rocks. They didn't. After a while the lights twinkled away. There's even been a watch kept over around San Antonio Bay, to the west. Nothing happened there."

"Those ships you mentioned," Slade remarked. "Were they spotted on stormy nights?"

The sheriff ruminated a moment. "Come to think of it, I believe they were," he replied. "Why?"

"Last night was stormy, and I distinctly saw the lights of a ship standing off-shore; she didn't put in. May have been just coincidence, but then again it may not. Of course there is less chance of detection on a bad night, which wide-loopers take into consideration."

"That's so," the sheriff conceded. "And you actually did for two of the devils? That's more than anybody else has been able to do. Not a bad beginning. I've a notion business is going to pick up. Wonder if they'll spot you for El Halcón, even maybe for a Ranger?"

"I'll settle for El Halcón," Slade replied. "I hope to keep my Ranger connections secret, at least for a while. Be better that way."

The sheriff nodded but looked dubious, as Captain Jim

McNelty often did when he and Slade discussed the matter.

Owing to his habit of working under cover as much as possible and often not revealing his Ranger identity, Walt Slade had built up a peculiar dual reputation. The smartest Ranger of them all, and he ain't scared of anything that walks, crawls or flies, said those who knew the truth. Just a blasted outlaw with too much savvy to get caught, so far, declared others, including some puzzled sheriffs and marshals.

Slade did nothing to correct this erroneous impression, although he was forced to admit that it laid him open to grave personal danger, as Captain Jim often pointed out. But Slade insisted that it afforded a much better chance of acquiring valuable information and that it was worth the risk.

"Let the owlhoots think I'm just one of their brand trying to horn in on some good thing they've started," he said. "Then they get careless and tip their hands."

"Uh-huh, and you'll end up getting your hand tipped by some trigger-happy deputy, or some gunslinger out to get a reputation by downing El Halcón, 'the fastest gunhand in the whole Southwest.' Oh, go ahead! Go ahead! I get sore tonsils arguing with you!"

So Slade continued to "go ahead" on the path of his choosing, satisfied with the present and giving little thought to the future.

"Well, suppose we go hunt up Doc Price and let him have a look at your head," Ross suggested. "You got a bad rap, and it shouldn't be neglected."

"Guess you're right," Slade conceded. "I don't think there is anything much to it, but it's better not to take chances."

As they walked along the street, Slade gestured toward a big and sprawling building to the right.

"Seems to me that one has acquired an addition since I was here last year," he remarked.

"It has," said the sheriff. "Used to be one of old Shanghai Pierce's slaughterhouses. Now it's Eldon Parr's packing establishment. Parr packs sheep meat."

"A good site for it, here," Slade commented. "Plenty of sheep in this section."

"Parr mostly brings his woollies in by ship," replied Ross. "Owns a couple of ranches over to the east, I understand. He bought local sheep when he came here, about four months back, but because of the blasted men of steel scare he can't depend on local deliveries. He's threatened to start a ranch hereabouts, which doesn't set too well with the cowmen—quite a bit of open range here which they use but don't own. They're scared that if he does bring in sheep he'll let them run wild over the range, and you know what that means. All the sheep in this section are owned by the Mexican herders down to the southwest, where the cowmen haven't any holdings."

Slade nodded his understanding. He knew what carelessly handled sheep would do to rangeland. The prophet Ezekiel knew what he was talking about when he wrote:

"Woe be to the shepherds of Israel . . . . Seemeth it a small thing unto you to have eaten up the good pasture, but ye must tread down with your feet the residue of your pastures? . . . "

That is just what sheep, carelessly handled, do. They kill more than they eat. They feed in compact masses, and their sharp chisel feet, driven by a hundred pounds of solid bone and flesh, cut even the roots of the grass to pieces. As a result, vegetation may be killed for years to come. The damage is even more serious in arid lands, where vegetation is essential to the conservation of moisture. Without vegetable life, rain is not absorbed but runs off the ground and cuts it into arroyos and ravines where nothing will grow. A range overstocked with cattle is in for trouble, sooner or later. With sheep, it is sooner.

Which is the reason for the bloody range wars fought in the West because of the encroaching woollies.

But Slade knew that experience had taught that sheep and cattle can be raised in the same section to the advantage of both; it is just a matter of proper handling. Steep and stony pastures that are worthless for cattle provide good grazing for sheep. Wise ranchers take advantage of this fact and profit thereby.

The flock owners of Mexican descent, who had held their land for generations, knew how to handle sheep properly and did handle them properly, keeping their charges constantly on the move, never allowing them to eat the grass down to the roots or otherwise damage it.

However, it was all too often different with unscrupulous owners out for quick profits and caring nothing for the welfare of others. So it was not remarkable that the cattlemen of the section looked askance on any plan to run sheep in and onto the open range.

"Parr is quite a gent, and he sure knows the packing business," Ross observed. "Well, here's Doc's place, and I reckon he's in."

Old Doc Price, who also knew Slade well, shook hands warmly and gestured him to a chair.

"Nicked again, eh?" he remarked as he undid the bandage. "Keep up at this rate and your head will end looking like a patchwork quilt. Hmmm! Not so bad. You did a good chore of padding and bandaging. A cleansing, a couple of stitches and a strip of plaster, and you'll be okay."

A few minutes later he stepped back and surveyed his handiwork.

"There, that'll hold you," he said. "Pull your hat down on that side and it won't even show. Fee? What fee? You go to hell!"

"We *were* going over to the Post Hole," admitted the sheriff. "Join us in a snort, Doc?"

"Not a bad idea," agreed Price. "Should be sort of exciting before the night's over, with El Halcón in town."

"That's what I'm scared of," groaned the sheriff. "Trouble just naturally follows him around."

After the doctor had cleaned and put away his instruments, they set out for the saloon in question. Dusk was sifting down through the still air. The bay was smoldering purple flecked with flashes of rose and gold. Far out on the water a ship was heading for port, the tips of her tall masts catching the last dying sunlight and beaconing it back in rays of amber. Port Lavaca crouched expectantly on its low bluff and awaited the night.

4

━━━━━━━━━━━━━━━━━━━━━━━━━━━━━━━━━━━━━━

THE POST HOLE WAS BIG, well lighted and boisterous. The bar was pretty well crowded, the orchestra already tuning up, the dance-floor girls gathered together, talking. Some of the gaming tables were occupied. A couple of roulette wheels were whirring, and the faro bank was going strong.

"Sort of lively for so early in the evening," Slade commented.

"Payday for the spreads and for most of the other workers hereabouts," Sheriff Ross explained. "They try to have 'em all hit together; good for business. Especially Doc's."

"But not conducive to peace and quiet," observed that worthy. "Well, here goes for that snort."

"And then something to eat," Slade suggested.

"I'm in favor of it," said Doc. "I'm gaunt as a gutted sparrow. And Neale is always hungry—can't get over his starvation days as a cowhand. Used to be so thin he couldn't cast a shadow. Fat and sleek, now that he's got his hand in the public till, but he still eats. Not that I'm complaining; I'm getting rich dosing him with stuff to take off some of the tallow. A pity he hasn't got stronger arms."

"How's that?" asked the sheriff, falling into the trap.

"So you could push yourself away from the table before your belly shoves against it," snorted Doc. "Fill 'em up, bartender."

The three repaired to a table, where they enjoyed a hearty meal. Afterwards they sat sipping coffee, and smoking and talking.

Frog-lip Fogarty, the owner, came over from the end of the bar to join them. Ross performed the introductions, and Fogarty shook hands with a firm grip. An expression of perplexity crossed his good-natured, big-mouthed face as he regarded Slade.

"Seems to me I ought to know you, cowboy," he said. "I've either seen you before or heard of somebody who looks like you."

"Lots of folks look alike," Slade replied noncommittally.

Frog-lip did not appear impressed. "Anyhow, I'm sorry to see you in such bad company," he sighed. "A sheriff and a doctor! All we need is an undertaker to make it perfect."

"And the chances are you'll need all three in this rum-hole before the night is over," the sheriff predicted. "I never knew it to fail."

"Could be," admitted Frog-lip. "The boys are apt to get a mite rambunctious after a while, but I've a notion I can quiet them down if I have to. Well, enjoy yourself, gents, I'll send over a drink." He sauntered back to the bar, his step lithe and quick for so bulky a man.

"Yes, he can usually quiet 'em down," conceded the sheriff. "A nice jigger, but he can be plenty salty if necessary, and he's got a couple of floor men of the same caliber."

The drinks were brought and placed beside the coffee cups. Doc and the sheriff downed theirs, the latter smacking his lips with appreciation. Slade left his untouched for the moment. His gaze was fixed on a rather striking appearing individual who had just entered.

"That's Eldon Parr I was telling you about," said the sheriff.

Eldon Parr was a big man with wide shoulders and abnormally long arms that hung loosely by his sides. He was good-looking in a rugged way, with craggy features, a thin-lipped but well-shaped mouth, and eyes of very light blue. His stride was assured, his bearing also assured, to the verge of arrogance. He wore clean overalls and a blue shirt open at the throat, but, unlike most of the gathering, no gun belt.

As Parr neared the bar, a big cowhand, more than half drunk, detached himself from a group and accosted him. Slade could not hear what was said, but the effect on Parr was galvanic. His hand lashed out, and the flat of it took the cowboy across the mouth, sending him reeling back. He tripped over his own feet, slammed into a table and hit the floor amid a shower of bottles and glasses. Spitting blood and curses, he scrambled to his feet. His right hand flickered down and up; a black muzzle lined with Parr's chest.

The room echoed to the crash of a shot. The cowboy gave a howl of pain and doubled up, gripping his blood-streaming hand between his knees. His gun, one butt plate knocked off, lay half across the room.

A long-barrelled Colt in each hand, one wisping smoke,

Walt Slade swept the suddenly hushed crowd with his cold eyes. After one swift glance he holstered his guns with the same effortless ease with which he had drawn them, sat down and raised his brimming glass to his lips with a hand that did not spill a drop.

Sheriff Ross let out a bellow of wrath. "Parr!" he thundered. "What the blankety-blank-blank do you mean by coming in here and slapping folks around! And as for you, Hodson, you came mighty, mighty close to having a cold-blooded killing to your credit. Parr isn't even heeled. You'd better both be thanking Slade here for what he saved you from. And if I hear any more out of either of you, I'll lock you up and throw the key away."

The words had a cooling effect on the antagonists. Sheriff Neale Ross was a cold proposition and known to be as good as his word.

"Guess you're right," groaned the puncher, tenderly cherishing his throbbing hand. "That big feller with you, too. But if you'd had half your teeth knocked loose, you wouldn't have felt so good, either." He shot a venomous look at Parr.

"I'm sorry, Hodson," said the latter. "I shouldn't have gone off half-cocked; but you shouldn't have said to me what you did."

"Guess that's right," conceded Hodson. "I'm sorry, too. And if you don't mind taking the left one—" He held it out, hesitantly. They shook hands.

"That's better," said the sheriff.

Doc Price lumbered across to the cowboy. "Let's have a look at that lunch hook," he said. "Nothing to it—just a hunk of meat knocked loose. Frog-lip, fetch the bandages and stuff you always keep handy."

A few minutes later the wound was dressed and bandaged. Somebody handed Hodson his fallen gun. He shook his head sadly over the smashed butt plate and holstered it.

"Both of you have one on the house and forget all about it," suggested Frog-lip, who was looking Slade up and down.

He saw a tall man, taller even than Eldon Parr, with broad shoulders and a deep chest that slimmed down to a lean, sinewy waist, and a face that went well with the splendid form, a face dominated by long black-lashed eyes of very pale gray, cold but with little devils of laughter lurking in their clear depths. The rather wide mouth, grin-quirked at the corners, relieved somewhat the tinge of fierceness evinced by the prominent, high-bridged nose above and the lean and powerful jaw and chin beneath. The pushed-back "J.B." revealed crisp, thick hair so black that a blue shadow seemed to lie upon it. An unusual and extremely handsome face, Frog-lip thought. The look of perplexity that he had worn was gone, replaced by one of understanding. He approached the table.

"Feller," he said in low tones, "betcha a hatful of pesos you ride a black horse."

"You'd win," Slade smiled.

"I knew it!" sighed Frog-lip. "I knew it! Didn't I say all this table needed was an undertaker to make it perfect. I'll send over another drink."

"Caught on quick, eh?" chuckled the sheriff as Frog-lip walked away. "Suppose somebody else will, too. Listen to the talk, will you!"

Slade had already overheard some of the remarks running from table to table and along the bar.

"Did you ever see such shooting! Those irons just happened in his hands. Hodson had already lined sights, and that feller pulled and blasted the hogleg clean across the room 'fore he could squeeze trigger! Who the devil is he, anyhow?"

"Dunno, but he's somebody. Huh! What's that? Are you sure? Wheee-e-w! The fastest gunhand in the whole Southwest! Now I believe it. Gentl-l-lemen, hush!"

The sheriff grinned. Doc Price chuckled. "Can't hide your light under a bushel, or a barn," he misquoted.

"So it would seem," Slade replied.

"Anyhow, you sure saved Eldon Parr's bacon," observed Ross.

"I'm not so sure," Slade said. "I think he would have missed the first shot, and Parr would have been all over him before he could pull trigger again. He's quick as a cat."

"Uh-huh, but I doubt he's that quick," said Ross.

Suddenly, from a table where heads were drawn together, came a bellow.

"And the singingest man in the whole Southwest, too! Hey, feller, give us a song. You don't have to shoot us, just sing us one and we'll crawl!"

Other voices took up the plea, until the room resounded with a chorus of requests. Sheriff Ross shook with laughter.

"Looks like you're elected, Walt," he chuckled. "Come on, give us one, and make everybody in here your friend for life. Here comes the orchestra leader, with a guitar. Those Mexicans of his all know you, but they're good at keeping tight *latigos* on their jaws and never would have given you away till you put the okay on it."

The orchestra leader was at the table, bowing and smiling and holding out the guitar.

"Please, *Capitán*," he pleaded. "When El Halcón sings, the stars pause to listen."

"Well, if you can stand it, I reckon I can," Slade acquiesced. He stood up.

Strutting proudly, the leader led the way to the little raised platform that accommodated the orchestra. With a low bow, he handed Slade the guitar and stepped back.

Slade ran his slender fingers over the strings of the instrument with crisp power. He glanced about, saw that the majority of the expectant crowd were cowhands. He smiled, flung back his black head and sang them a gay but wistful love song of the range:

> Night! and the sky's wide glory.
> A whisper of wind in the sage!
> With the high stars telling a story,
> As plain as the printed page!

> Night! and the gray trail flowing
> Under the moon's pale beams!
> The light of the campfire glowing;
> Night! and a girl—and—dreams!

And as the great golden baritone-bass pealed and thundered, a cathedral hush fell over the crowded saloon. No drink was poured, no card turned. The roulette wheels hung motionless. The dancers paused and stood almost at attention, in impulsive salute.

Just a simple little song of simple words, composed beside some lonely campfire or around a restless herd, but rendered into a thing of sublime beauty by the magic of a great voice.

The song ended in a lingering breath of melody, and Slade stood smiling at his entranced audience.

The hush lingered for a moment, then was broken by a storm of applause and shouts for another.

Slade gave them several more before restoring the guitar to its owner and returning to the table. For an instant his glance lingered on Eldon Parr, standing erect and commanding by the bar. From the moment he had entered the room, his expression had not changed. During the hectic encounter with the cowhand his face had remained impassive as a deal board. Only his eyes seemed to burn as they rested on El Halcón's tall form. After Slade was seated, he strolled to the table.

"May I?" he said, nodding to a vacant chair.

"Sit down, Eldon, and have a drink," Sheriff Ross invited hospitably. "How was that for singing? Ever hear the beat of it? I never did."

"And I doubt if you ever will," replied Parr. He turned to Slade. "You are to be congratulated on your rare gift. And, incidentally, I wish to thank you for what you did in my behalf. I thought for an instant I was going to get an air hole in my hide."

"I doubt if he would have pulled trigger, but I thought it best not to take chances," Slade answered.

"I am very glad you thought so," Parr returned dryly. "I am not very adept in the use of a gun, so I seldom carry one. Hodson, I understand, is. And I have noted that a man who *is* adept in handling one is usually quick to use it."

Slade nodded but did not otherwise comment. He was confident in his own mind that Hodson *did* intend to use the gun he drew.

"Eldon, just what did Al Hodson say to you that set you off so?" asked the sheriff.

"It was not what he said, but the manner in which he said it," replied Parr. "Tonal inflection can carry a more stinging impact than words. What he said was, 'All of a sudden this place is smelling mighty strong of sheep.' The words alone could have meant little, but the implication was plain."

"I see," said the sheriff. Walt Slade, while not appearing to do so, abruptly took a stronger interest in Eldon Parr; his manner of expressing himself, the Ranger thought, was a trifle out of the ordinary.

"Sheep!" growled the sheriff. "The blattin' varmints always can be counted on to kick up a ruckus where there's open range. We can do without them here—the herders down to the south have all that's needed. Let them handle them."

"Sheriff," Eldon Parr said, "if I decide to run sheep onto the open range here I will do so, despite opposition. If the land is open range for cattle, there is no reason why it shouldn't be open range to sheep."

Parr spoke calmly, without raising his voice, but Slade was convinced he meant exactly what he said. He was impressed with the force of the man's personality and believed that opposition would not deter him from any set purpose.

"You'll be looking for trouble if you do run 'em in," Sheriff Ross warned.

"I think," Eldon Parr replied deliberately, "that I am competent to take care of any trouble that comes my way. Good night, gentlemen." He rose to his feet, and with a nod, left the saloon.

5

SHERIFF Ross cocked an eye at Slade.

"Well, what do you think of him?"

"A hard man, but with a weakness, perhaps his only one," Slade replied.

"What's that?" the sheriff asked curiously.

"Temper," Slade said. "He let it get away from him tonight. Temper clouds the judgment. Had he been his normal cold, practical self, he would not have struck Hodson as he did."

"You mean he woulda let Al get away with it?"

Slade shook his head. "No, he would have struck with his fist, with all his weight behind it. Then Hodson would have been in no condition to pull a gun or anything else. Hodson undoubtedly has an uncontrollable temper, especially when he is drinking. Parr should have taken that into account, especially as he was not packing a gun, and made sure Hodson would not be capable of retaliation, if he felt he must resent the remark. As it was, he merely stung him and came close to getting his come-uppance in consequence."

"I've a notion you're right," conceded the sheriff. "Loco galoots, both of them. How about some more coffee?"

As they sat sampling the steaming cups, he suddenly uttered a sharp exclamation.

"Blazes! I'm glad Parr left when he did. Here comes Phil Waring. If Parr was still here, there'd likely be more trouble. There is bad blood between those two."

The newcomer was a tall, rawboned young man with sparkling black eyes, a tight mouth and a long cleft chin. He swaggered to the bar and ordered a drink, his glance sweeping the room as if in quest of somebody. Slade noticed that when he settled down to his drink, his eyes were studying the gathering as reflected in the backbar mirror.

"Yep, those two don't get along," repeated the sheriff. "A few months back, Parr had Waring arrested for trespassing. Said he was snooping around his packing plant, likely planning to set fire to it. Could be. Waring's got no use for sheep in any form and don't make no bones about saying so. The judge let him off with a lecture, but he hasn't forgot and holds it against Parr."

Slade eyed Waring with awakened interest. "Cattleman?" he asked.

"That's right," replied Ross. "Owns the W Diamond up to the northwest. That is, he and his sister Marie own it together. Inherited it from their dad, old Wallis Waring, who died about five years back. It's a good holding. Al Hodson is one of his hands. Look, they're talking together."

For several moments the pair were deep in conversation. Waring's gaze shifted to the table occupied by Slade and his companions. Abruptly he turned and walked to the table, his swagger more pronounced. Pausing, he let his glittering eyes rest on Slade's face. He nodded, not unpleasantly.

"Want to say much obliged, feller, for keeping that loco centipede from killing Eldon Parr," he said, in a rumbling but not unmusical voice.

"Would have thought you'd have been glad if he did," snorted the sheriff, regarding Waring with scant favor.

"Nope," Waring returned, his voice cheerful. "Nope, I want that pleasure myself. Would have felt plumb bad if Hodson had beat me to it."

He turned his back on the glaring sheriff and walked back to the bar.

"Blankety-blanked horned toad!" sputtered the angry peace officer. "He meant it!"

"I've a notion he did," Slade agreed, the little devils of laughter leaping to the fore. There was a comical side to the sheriff's wrath.

"He's been in trouble before," growled Ross. "Plugged a dealer through the shoulder in a poker game in the Occidental, down the street, and busted furniture. Got fined for that one. Oh, he's a hell-raiser for fair. Liable to be mixed up in anything."

"That was a dangerous thing for him to say before witnesses," Slade said seriously. "If he should happen to have a ruckus with Parr and kill him, he might well find himself facing a first degree murder charge based on premeditation."

"Maybe they'll plug each other," Doc Price remarked hopefully. "I don't like either one of 'em. Parr is too darned uppity, and Waring is a pest."

"I don't see how a nice girl like Marie could have such an ornery rapscallion for a brother," the sheriff complained.

"Well," said Doc, "I understand that old Wallis himself was

a good deal of a ripsnorter when he was young. Reckon it's in the blood. But a feller could get by with more in those days. Not much law hereabouts then other than what a man packed on his hip."

"Hasn't changed too much for the better," Ross replied morosely.

Doc Price glanced at the clock over the bar. "Well," he said, "you young hellions can stay up all night if you want to, but I'm going to bed."

"And I'm going to follow your example," Slade said. "I didn't sleep too well last night, everything considered."

"Come on over to my place," Doc invited. "I got plenty of room, and it isn't bad for bachelor quarters. Plenty to eat in the house, too, and even if I do say so, I'm a pretty good cook. You'll be more comfortable than in one of those flea sacks they call hotels."

"Be glad to," Slade accepted. "See you tomorrow, Ross."

"Okay," the sheriff nodded. "Got to keep an eye on the notorious El Halcón. Glad, anyhow, it won't be at an inquest, which is more than I hoped for a bit ago. I'll stick around here a while in case something else busts loose."

"The presence of the majesty of the law should keep the boys on their good behavior," said Doc. "Come on, Walt, he's just using that for an excuse to get drunk."

Before lying down on the comfortable bed in the room Doc Price assigned him, Slade cleaned and oiled his guns and did some serious thinking. Looked like there was more to the chore handed him than had appeared on the surface. Not only was there a shrewd and salty outlaw bunch operating in the section, which presented a problem, there was a row between two prominent citizens and the probability of a grand cattle-sheep conflict in the making. If Eldon Parr made good his threat and ran woollies onto the open range, the cowmen of the section would be up in arms. Parr must know that and, Slade believed, would make provisions against it. Parr struck him as a man who would not be deterred by the possibility of trouble.

Meanwhile, the herders to the southwest, who handled their sheep properly on their own land, would be caught in the middle.

First, the grotesque "men of steel" must be handled. Slade believed he saw a way to take care of that angle. Once more his El Halcón reputation might well stand him in good stead. Worth trying, anyhow. He went to bed in a cheerful frame of mind.

He was still cheerful when he awoke late the following morning.

"Figured you needed your rest, so I didn't bother you," said Doc. "Come on and eat."

After enjoying an excellent breakfast prepared by Doc Price, Slade repaired to the sheriff's office. When he arrived there, he found Ross had a visitor—a slender, dark-faced and exceedingly handsome middle-aged man who appeared mad as a hornet.

Don Miguel Lopez—although Texas-born as was his father before him, he was still accorded the courtesy title of *Don*—was angry, and with cause. Miguel Lopez was not a man to be frightened by wild yarns of iron-shirted riders or affected by local superstitions. With his herders, however, most of whom were Mexicans, it was a different story. Lopez, Sheriff Ross informed Slade, after performing the introductions, was the biggest sheep owner in the section and also raised cattle, improved stock that brought top prices.

"I tell you, Neale, it goes beyond all patience," he said. "Those infernal masqueraders have been scouting my place, and my herders are scared stiff. They say they fear no mortal foe—and they speak truth—but who can give face to the Powers of Darkness? In vain I reason with them. They are loyal to me in all else, but they refuse absolutely to drive a flock to town. Eldon Parr will take a flock if I can get it here, gladly, but how to get it here! I can't very well ask my *vaqueros* to handle the chore. As you know, nearly all of them are Texas-born and have no more use for sheep than any other Texas cowboy. In addition, they have their hands full keeping an eye on my cows. I don't know what the devil to do if you don't clean out that gang of owlhoots, for that's all they are, brush-popping border scum."

Slade, who had listened intently to what Lopez had to say, spoke for the first time.

"They're more than brush-popping scum," he remarked. "Somebody connected with the outfit has brains, and imagination, both attributes not common to the average owlhoot."

"I fear you may be right, Mr. Slade," Lopez replied gloomily. "Which certainly doesn't make the picture look any brighter."

"No, but it is significant," Slade said. Lopez' brows drew together, in the manner of a man trying to recall something to memory.

"Mr. Slade," he said, "somehow your name has a familiar

ring. I seem to have heard it before, somewhere, in some connection."

"Possibly," Slade conceded. "I understand that the majority of your herders are Mexican-born."

"That's so," nodded Lopez.

"Probably from the Rio Grande river villages."

Lopez nodded again. "Most of those born in Texas are also from the villages on this side of the river," he added. "Why?"

"It may be important," Slade replied briefly. For some moments he sat silent, while the other watched him expectantly. Finally he glanced at the sheriff and nodded.

Ross chuckled. "Mig," he said, "did you ever hear of El Halcón?"

"Why, of a certainty, El Halcón—the fearless, the just. Who has not? I—"

He ceased speaking and his eyes widened. "Ha!" he exclaimed, "I have it! No wonder your name had a familiar ring, Mr. Slade! *You* are El Halcón!"

"Been called that," Slade admitted smilingly.

Don Miguel heaved a deep sigh, a sigh that was undoubtedly one of relief. "I believe," he said deliberately, "that my sheep will be driven to market, after all."

"Yes," Slade smiled, "I think they will. Suppose we ride down to your place; I wish to have a talk with your herders. We should be able to make it by shortly after dark."

"Assuredly," said Lopez, rising to his feet. "We will start at once, and *gracias*, Mr. Slade, *gracias!* It is most kind of you."

"Have a little personal interest in the matter," Slade replied, tapping his bandaged forehead. "I'd like to meet the rest of those gents in tin shirts, especially with a bunch of good fighters at my back. Let's go."

"I'll come and pick up the bodies," Sheriff Ross called cheerfully after them as they left the office. "Good hunting!"

6

As THEY WERE GETTING the rigs on their horses, Slade asked, *"Don* Miguel, just what do you know about the so-called men of steel?"

"Very little," the other replied. "It is as difficult for me to obtain information as it is for the sheriff. You see, I am of Spanish blood, but that is about all Mexican that I can claim. My herders and the *peones* are evasive when I question them. They don't look on me as one of them. Had I a leavening of *indio* blood, it might be different, but to them I am just an ignorant all-white who does not understand. As Ross no doubt told you, they fear to talk, saying, or at least implying that there are ears listening in the dark beyond the dark and unheard voices ready to report all that is said. They are less fearful of property loss or death than they are of demon retribution handed out by the awful denizens of the unseen world, of whom they believe the men of steel are a part. So when I try to learn something, I am met by either a shrug of the shoulders or evasive generalities that mean nothing."

"I see," Slade said thoughtfully. "I think," he continued, "that there will be a little change of heart on the part of your herders and the *peones.* Sweep the cobwebs out of their brains and they'll be the same tough fighters against the men of steel as they are against ordinary owlhoots."

"That's so," Lopez agreed, adding gloomily, "but so far I haven't done much of a job of sweeping."

"Perhaps you didn't use the right broom," Slade smiled. "Fear is a strong emotion, but faith is stronger. The methods we will employ will be something in the nature of fighting fire with fire; we'll see who can set the biggest blaze."

"I think I can provide the answer to that," *Don* Miguel said gently. "The *peones* say that El Halcón is one upon whom the hand of God has rested, sent to do His work in the world, who can give front to all the Powers of Darkness."

Slade's cold eyes were suddenly all kindness. "I hope I won't forfeit their trust," he replied.

"You won't," *Don* Miguel declared, with emphasis.

They were several miles from town when they saw a horseman approaching from the south. As he drew near, Slade recognized Phil Waring, the boisterous young owner of the W Diamond ranch. Waring waved a hand in greeting.

"Hello, Lopez, how are you?" he called. "Howdy, Mr. Slade, where'd you run into this old coot? Don't mind him. He's all right, even if he does raise sheep."

"How are you, Phil?" Lopez asked, his smile pleasant. "What are you doing down this way?"

"Oh, just riding around," Waring replied evasively. "Heading for your holding?"

"That's right," Lopez answered. "Mr. Slade has consented to be my guest for a few days."

"Everybody to their taste, as the herder said when he kissed the sheep," Waring said cheerfully. "If he can stand the smell of the blattin' woollies, maybe he'll make out. Come to think of it, you don't keep 'em close to the house; reckon you can't stand it yourself."

"There are worse smells," Lopez returned.

"Guess that's right," Waring conceded, his face darkening. "Take Eldon Parr, for instance; he out-stinks any sheep that ever grew wool."

"I wish you'd forget your feud with Parr," Lopez said. "It will only bring you trouble in one way or another. Nothing is ever gained from holding a grudge."

Waring did not look convinced. "Be seeing you," he said. "Glad to have run into you again, Mr. Slade."

With a wave of his hand, he rode on, and did not look back. Lopez turned in the saddle to follow his retreating figure with his gaze.

"A wild young man, but I can't help but like him," he remarked. "Lots of people do not think at all well of him, and there are hints—but I don't spread gossip. I wonder what he was doing down here?"

"He didn't say," Slade replied thoughtfully. He was wondering a little himself.

As they rode, Slade carefully studied the terrain over which they passed, wishing to familiarize himself with its salient points. For he knew it would take two full days at least to move a flock from Lopez' place to Port Lavaca. Which meant a night camp, possibly two. And he gathered that at night camps herders had been slain and their flocks wide-looped.

When they reached the point, shortly before sundown, where Slade had had the run-in with the two men of steel, he pulled up and surveyed his surroundings for some minutes, then nodded with satisfaction.

"Right here we'll probably make our camp," he told Lopez. "Yes, this is a very good spot for it. May mean a second camp before we reach town, but I've a notion it will pay off."

The ride was without untoward happenings, but it was long after dark when they reached *Don* Miguel's spacious *hacienda*, built in the Spanish style and situated in a grove of ancient oaks. A wrangler, who was formally introduced to Shadow, took charge of the horses.

After making sure his guest was comfortable in the spacious living room, Lopez immediately repaired to the bunkhouse occupied by the herders. A *criado*, who bowed low to Slade after an instant of wide-eyed surprise, brought the Ranger a cup of steaming coffee. Slade relaxed in an easy chair and awaited his host's return.

Lopez did return shortly, chuckling.

"The news created quite a stir," he told Slade. "The boys will all be assembled in front of the veranda, awaiting you, right after breakfast tomorrow morning. They're very much excited. I don't think you'll have any trouble making them see things your way. Well, let's go eat; been a long time since breakfast."

It had been, but as Slade viewed the meal that a worshipful cook and an equally worshipful *criado* set before him, he felt it was worth going foodless since morning to be in a condition to do full justice to it. The old servant who passed the dishes beamed with pleasure at the havoc wrought, and so did the cook. Both were old men of Mexican-Indio blood, usually impassive and unemotional, but tonight they were positively exuberant.

"Mr. Slade," *Don* Miguel said when they returned to the living room to smoke and talk over final cups of fragrant coffee, "it is marvelous the impression you make on people. Yes, marvelous. I am indeed honored to have El Halcón as my guest."

"Thank you, *Don* Miguel," Slade replied simply.

When Slade appeared on the veranda the following morning, the herders, all eight of them mature men, were already present, looking eager and expectant. In another group were the *vaqueros*, ten in number. They were mostly young, and wiry and active as panthers. Slade liked the looks of both groups. He addressed the herders.

"*Amigos*, they tell me you are afraid of a bunch of *ladrones* in tin shirts. I don't believe it. First, however, I want to talk a little about those men of steel whose steel isn't steely enough to stop a bullet. I understand that the herders who have been slain met their death by way of .45 slugs. Now is it reasonable to believe that spirits would resort to such prosaic methods? Wouldn't they be more apt to employ thunderbolts?"

He paused. The herders looked bewildered, but nodded their heads in agreement.

"Also," Slade continued, "I have learned that the raids always took place on dark and stormy nights, when it is easier to wide-loop critters and the raids can be conducted with less chance of the raiders being detected. Wind and darkness provide good cover for run-of-mine rustlers with the forked end down and a hat on top. But would ghostly horsemen such as it is claimed have been seen, who have the ability to vanish away at will and snatch flocks into the clouds, who are impervious to such small items as the hot end of a passing bullet or the constructive qualities of a noosed sisal rope around the windpipe, have any qualms about being detected in their nefarious activities? Doesn't seem reasonable, does it?"

Again there were nods of agreement, more emphatic this time.

"All right," Slade said, letting the full force of his steady gray eyes rest on the faces of the herders. "Now I have something to tell you. The other night I killed two of those 'spirit' horsemen. Their armor couldn't stop my bullets. And before I downed them both, they gave me this to remember them by—" He touched his bandaged head and added impressively, "And they didn't do it with a thunderbolt or a devil's pitchfork; they did it with hot lead."

The herders stared at him, muttering together.

"All right," he repeated. "Very shortly a flock is going to be driven to Port Lavaca, despite the so-called men of steel. Who among you have the will to follow El Halcón? Let them raise their hands."

Instantly eight hands shot into the air.

"Where El Halcón leads, we will follow," a voice called. "El Halcón, the friend of the lowly, of the wronged and the oppressed, fears naught in this world or the next, because his heart is clean. Sí, we will follow!"

"I thought you would," Slade said, with a smile. "If those *ladrones* in tin shirts try to interfere with us, we'll use .45 caliber can openers on them."

There was a roar of laughter. Slade held out his hand and the herders pressed forward to shake it, albeit diffidently.

Slade noticed that the *vaqueros* had their heads together. One, whom he learned was Sebastian Hernandez, the range boss, detached himself from the group and approached *Don Miguel.*

"*Patrón,*" he said, "five men are sufficient to care for and guard the *ganado.* The other five of us would fain ride with El Halcón. We will cast lots as to who is to go and who is to stay."

Lopez glanced questioningly at Slade, who nodded. "The more the better," he said, and turned to the herders.

"Get your flock ready to move when I give the word," he said, and glanced at the sky, which was hazy. "Very likely tomorrow will be the day. I want each man to pack two blankets and bring along a pair of overalls, a shirt and a hat, and a sack of straw. And I also want an old and dependable horse accustomed to night guard work. Everything understood? Okay. Be seeing you, *amigos.*

"Incidentally," he added to Lopez, "have the *vaqueros* dress as herders. Whoever got that bunch together and is the head of it has plenty of savvy. If the *vaqueros* wore their regular riding costume, it might be noted and he might smell a rat."

"I will attend to it," Lopez promised. He shook his head as they entered the house together.

"Wonderful!" he exclaimed. "With a few words you did what I could not do for all my persuasion and promises of reward. The herders are brave men, once the cloud of superstition is swept from their minds. They will fight like demons at your behest. I think that if the men of steel attempt to raid the flock they will get a lesson they will not soon forget. That is, if any are left alive to remember."

"I hope so," Slade said. "But it's a salty outfit, and whoever is heading it has plenty of wrinkles on his horns. One little slip and it can well be us instead of them."

"I have no fears as to the outcome," said Lopez. "In fact, I'd like to ride with you."

Slade shook his head. "I think it is better for you to remain here and be in evidence should anybody be keeping tabs on the place," he decided. "We don't want them to get unduly suspicious and suspect that a trap is being set for them."

"Doubtless you are right," Lopez conceded. "When do you plan to move?"

"Depends on the weather," Slade replied. "I want a stormy day and night, if possible, and from the looks of the sky we might have that tomorrow. From appearances I'd say a storm is brewing out in the Gulf and should hit here during the next twenty-four hours or so, that is, if it doesn't happen to veer, as Gulf storms have a habit of doing."

Slade spent the afternoon riding over the spread with *Don* Miguel. He quickly decided it was a good holding, well watered and grassed and kept in fine condition. There were thousands of sheep and a good herd of cattle. He congratulated Lopez on the excellence of his property.

"Yes, I am comfortably fixed," the other returned. "But I have many poor relations, and there is always somebody else in need of help. I seldom have much ready money on hand, especially at this time of the year. Getting a flock to market will be a great help right now."

Slade nodded his understanding; his regard for Miguel Lopez had risen mightily, and he resolved that the flock in question would get to market, no matter who tried to stop it.

The haze thickened as the afternoon wore on. Through it the sun shone a weird magenta color. No leaf stirred. The grassheads stood stiffly erect. A dead calm had fallen.

"Storm coming, all right," Slade said. "From the looks of things, I'd say it's liable to be a real one; I know the signs. Well, that's what I hoped for."

Returning to the ranchhouse, Slade made sure everything was in readiness for an early start the following morning. He found the herders cheerful and confident. The five *vaqueros* who had won the toss-up, one being Sebastian Hernandez, the range boss, looked on the coming trip as a schoolboy looks on a holiday. They were a different caliber from the herders—more intelligent, more apt to scoff at all superstition. Slade was confident they did not consider the men of steel to be supernatural beings and were anxious to come to grips with them. Even their antipathy for sheep did not deter them.

"We will keep to the windward side of the stench," said Hernandez. "The *pastores* do not need our help to handle the flock."

During the night the wind rose, blowing in fitful gusts from the northwest. Another period of calm followed. Then it began blowing again, a steady and slowly strengthening blast from the southeast. Yes, another storm was bellowing in from the Gulf. Slade eyed the overcast sky of morning with satisfaction.

7

■>=<>=<>=<>=<>=<>=<>=<>=<>=<>=<>=<>=<>=<>=<>=<>=<>=■

SHORTLY AFTER the gray daybreak the flock got under way. Overhead the cloud wrack flowed out of the southeast, a leaden canopy that seemed to press down on the earth like a giant waterfall. The wind, slowly increasing in violence, developed a hollow moan. A wild day and an equally wild night appeared in the making.

The sheep, docile creatures in excellent condition, walked steadily, covering ground much faster than they appeared to. A *vaquero*, garbed as a herder, led a mild-eyed old horse, saddled and bridled.

Slade rode well in front of the flock, Hernandez, the range boss, beside him. The Ranger constantly scanned the trail ahead and the terrain over which they passed. The range boss was also vigilant and alert.

Hernandez was intelligent and Mission-educated. He spoke good colloquial English and was equally fluent in Spanish. He chuckled as he glanced back at the *vaqueros*, who were riding with the herders.

"I think my *muchachos* are less allergic to the odor of sheep than they claim to be," he said. "I think *they* were just a trifle dubious of the men of steel. Such things seem absurd viewed from a nineteenth century viewpoint, but to the more ignorant of my people they are very real. My people, many of them, live in the past. And the legend of the men of steel is very old, older than the Mexico of today. The ancient Aztecs who followed the Toltecs in what is now Mexico believed that their Hiawatha would some day return, coming from the black waters, as they called the sea. And they believed he would be white. That is why the Aztecs at first welcomed the invading Spaniards and treated them with reverence. They came from the black water, and they were white. So they must be from the spirit world."

He paused to light a husk cigarette and then continued.

"It did not take the Aztecs long to become disillusioned, but the legend persisted, and persists to this day. The legend of

the men of steel who would return and rule the world is still
very much alive. So when men who appeared to be clad in
medieval armor suddenly appeared, it is not remarkable that
they were viewed with terror by men who otherwise are brave
enough. The herders, and many others, feared to resist them,
dreading the awful retribution which would be inflicted on
them by the Powers of Darkness. Death was preferable to an
eternity of indescribable suffering."

"And some smart gent well versed in history and legend
saw opportunity and proceeded to cash in on it," Slade observed. "Well, it has occurred before, in many parts of the
world."

"That is so," agreed Hernandez. "But the play on superstition may turn out to be a two-edged sword. Take yourself, for
example, The *peones* of the river villages, the herders and
many others firmly believe that you have been touched by the
hand of *El Dios*, and because of that the spirit world has no
power over you. So they will follow you blindly and without
fear. Being under your protection, they believe that they also
are immune."

"And what do you believe, Sebastian?" Slade asked laughingly.

"I believe," the other returned gravely, "that the *peones*
and the herders are right. For any man who lives an honorable
and upright life and dedicates that life to the service of others
is touched by God's hand and is under His protection. And
no real harm can come to him no matter how great the danger
seems to be."

"Thank you, Sebastian," Slade said, and his cold eyes were
suddenly very warm indeed.

They rode on in silence. Slade's attention was fixed on a
range of low, brush-covered hills that started up abruptly some
seven or eight hundred yards to the north. Twice he saw what
appeared to be a moving shadow among the shadows.

"Sebastian," he said, "there's somebody pacing us up there
on those rises. He's trying to keep under cover but isn't doing
a very good job of it. I believe they are going to come to our
lure and will attempt something after we make camp tonight."

"I hope so," Hernandez replied cheerfully. "I never shot a
ghost, and I want to see what effect my bullets will have on
one. But your eyesight is amazing. I also have been watching
those hills and saw nothing. You are sure?"

"Yes, I'm sure," Slade replied. "There it is again, just a
flicker against the growth. He's keeping tabs on us, all right."

Hernandez stared northward and shook his head in admiration.

"I can't see a thing," he confessed. "How the devil do you do it?"

"Perhaps I've had rather more experience at this sort of thing," Slade replied. "Men who ride the border of outlaw land learn to see and hear what others do not."

Hernandez gave a derisive snort. "Outlaw land!" Then his eyes grew pensive, and he shot a keen look at his companion.

"Hmmm!" he said. "I wonder?"

"Don't wonder out loud," Slade smiled, having a pretty good notion of what the other was thinking.

"I won't," the range boss promised, "but I sure am wondering."

The day continued stormy, with the steady blast roaring up from the southeast and with occasional splatters of rain. The sheep had to face the wind, which retarded their progress. They were bleating querulously by the time the brush-and-grass-grown rise where Slade had had the run-in with the men of steel was reached.

"This will be it," the Ranger told the others. "Be dark before long—already getting gloomy. Here we'll make camp, at the edge of the brush Plenty of grass for the woolies over to the right. Okay, you know what to do, Everybody get busy. First get a fire going and make ready to cook. A surrounding and some hot coffee will help a lot."

"A man always shoots better on a full belly," Hernandez remarked. The others chuckled.

The tired sheep began nibbling grass. The horses grazed contentedly, veering away from the flock. A meal was cooked and eaten with the appetite of hungry men. Afterwards cigarettes were rolled and smoked. Overhead the wind boomed, but the thick stand of growth minimized its force below. The sky was black as ink, the night very dark.

"Made to order for us," Slade observed. "And I suppose those hellions think it's made to order for them, too. Well, we'll see about that. Time for everybody to move; we won't take chances here in the firelight too long. Pile green wood on the fire so it'll smolder and not give out much light."

The order was obeyed. The flames died down to a feeble flicker. The shadows drew closer. The herders and the *vaqueros* got busy around the fire. Soon blankets wrapped around bundles of twigs and branches were in place, very satisfactorily simulating sleeping men.

"Look more like herders than herders themselves," said Hernandez. "Only they smell better."

"You're no perfume of the rose yourself," came the indignant retort. Hernandez chuckled and placed a bundle of dry wood handy. The old horse, on its back a hunched and nodding figure that looked exactly like a weary night guard, paced slowly and sedately around the huddled flock, as it had done many a time around a cud-chewing herd. From time to time it paused to crop a little grass, then ambled on, as it would do all night long if nothing bothered it.

At the edge of the growth, the herders and *vaqueros*, the spare blankets over their shoulders, lounged comfortably against tree trunks. Slade stood a little apart, vigilantly alert, straining his ears to catch any sound above the steady clamor of the wind.

The hours passed slowly and tediously. Slade did not expect anything to happen before nearly midnight, but he couldn't afford to gamble on it. Their hope of coming through the venture successfully and unscathed depended on the element of surprise. If the raiders suspected what they were up against, they would make provisions against it and the hunter might well become the hunted. So he schooled himself to patience, and waited. The herders were growing a bit restless, but a sharp command spoken in a low voice quieted them.

Finally Slade heard the sound for which he had been waiting—the clash of a horse's iron on a stone. A moment later he could make out the soft clump of hoofs on the muddy trail. The sound came from the east and was very faint. Only the ears of El Halcón could have caught it.

"Get set," he whispered to his companions. "They've pulled up at the edge of the brush to the east. Something will break any minute now. Hold your fire till I give the word."

Dead silence, other than the warring of the elements, resumed. Slade tensed expectantly, every sense strained to hairtrigger alertness.

With the suddenness of a thunderclap the silence was shattered to shards. Shattered by a blast of gunfire. The figure on the horse's back lurched and swayed. The horse snorted and went away from there, the figure reeling drunkenly, a perfect simulacrum of a badly wounded man managing to stay in the hull. The blanket rolls about the smoldering fire twitched and jerked as bullets hammered them, then lay without sound or movement.

There was a long moment of tingling suspense. Then into the circle of faint firelight crept four figures. The herder standing next to Slade gasped as the flicker glinted on metal breastplates and caps. He touched the frightened man's shoulder with a reassuring hand. Then he stared intently at the figures creeping toward the blanket rolls.

Something wasn't as it should be. His mind worked at racing speed to counteract the unexpected. He stepped forward half a pace and his voice rolled forth.

"Elevate! You're covered!"

The men of steel jerked around spasmodically. Slade caught a gleam of shifted metal, and both his guns let go with a crash. The growth quivered to the roar as all the herders seemed to fire at once.

Down went the four men of steel, like automatons held erect on a single severed string. The herders whooped with triumph. Slade's voice rang out again.

"Back! Back into the brush! Move! Farther back!"

The command was obeyed without question, and not an instant too soon. From farther along the growth came another bellow of gunfire. Slugs ripped through twigs and branches in the space they had occupied a moment before.

Wheeling about, Slade fired at the flashes as swiftly as he could pull trigger; the herders joined in.

A wailing curse echoed the reports, and another. Then a voice boomed a command. There followed a prodigious crashing in the brush and the thud of hoofs on the trail.

Slade groped to where he had leaned his Winchester against a convenient trunk, seized it and raced to the edge of the growth. He caught a fleeting glimpse of a compact body of horsemen riding madly eastward. Before he could line sights, the darkness swallowed them. He emptied the rifle in their general direction, but with little hope of scoring a hit. The herders blazed away merrily till he called a halt.

"They've gone," he said. "Let's see what we bagged. Easy, now; if one is only wounded, he could be dangerous."

However, there was no need for caution; the four raiders were dead, riddled with bullets.

Hernandez threw dry wood on the fire. It blazed up with plenty of light. Slade bent over one of the still forms.

"Look!" he said disgustedly. "Sheets of tin wrapped around their chests and laced in the back! And tin caps! There are your men of steel. Don't look very steely now, do they?"

The herders swore in two languages, glaring at the bodies. "*Capitán*, we were fools," one said. "But we will be fools no longer. Do you think the others might come back?" he added hopefully.

"Not them," Slade replied. "They got a bellyful. I think we nicked one or two of them."

"How did you catch on that these four weren't all of them?" Hernandez asked.

"There was too much shooting in the beginning for just four men," Slade replied. "They were smart, all right. Held back a reserve in case something went haywire."

"And if it hadn't been for your quick thinking, some of us would have gotten it," Hernandez declared. "*Muchachos,* I guess we should say *gracias* to El Halcón for being alive."

"*Sí,*" was the answer. "Those who ride with El Halcón do not die; it is others who die, like these *ladrones.*"

"Well, I guess that settles the men of steel, at least so far as our herders are concerned," said Hernandez.

"Yes, it means the end of that myth, but it doesn't mean the end of a smart and salty outlaw bunch," Slade reminded him. "There were a dozen or more that skalleyhooted. They'll get over their scare, and this setback won't stop them from operating. I think the men of steel masquerade is over, but we've still got to look for trouble in the section so long as they are mavericking around. Well, we made a start, anyhow. Think I'll collect me a souvenir."

He reached down, gripped one of the tin shirts with his steely fingers and ripped it down the front, the soft metal tearing easily. He folded it carefully into a compact square and stowed it in his saddle pouch.

There was nothing outstanding about the dead outlaws so far as Slade could see. They were of a type common enough to the border country. Under their "armor" they wore conventional rangeland garb. Their pockets revealed nothing of significance other than a rather large sum of money, which Slade told Hernandez to divide among his men.

"Now suppose we see if we can locate their horses," he suggested. "They should be somewhere close, unless they followed the others."

With dry branches for torches, they quickly located the four horses grazing along the edge of the growth. Two bore HF Bar brands, the other two a Triangle A and a Four Dot, respectively.

"The HF Bar is an east Texas brand, Neches River country; I'm not sure about the others," Slade commented. "Means nothing, the chances are; horses can be bought, traded or stolen."

However, he carefully memorized the brands against possible future need.

With Hernandez accompanying him, Slade scouted along the trail to the east for some distance but discovered no more bodies. Evidently none of the fleeing outlaws had been seriously wounded.

"Well, now we'll take a chance on a little sleep," he told his companion. "I've a notion the storm is going to blow itself out before morning. We'll use those horses to pack the bodies to town with us. The sheriff can put them on exhibition. Somebody might recognize them. First, though, we'll run down the night guard horse and get the rigged-on dummy off so he'll be comfortable."

They had no difficulty retrieving the horse in question. Having gotten over his scare, he had returned to the grassland and was nosing about, the straw-stuffed shirt and overalls hanging lopsided from the saddle.

8

THE MORNING did dawn beautifully bright and clear. The wind had died to a gentle breeze, the sunshine was golden, the sky deep blue. The sheep, critters that took things in stride and had been little disturbed by the hullabaloo of the night before, marched along sturdily. The old night guard horse, freed of his burden, trudged contentedly in the rear. The bodies of the dead outlaws flopped grotesquely across the saddles of their mounts, and nobody paid them any mind. The herders and *vaqueros* chattered gaily and swore amiably at one another. It was in the nature of a triumphant march with the victors loaded with spoils in the shape of the money taken from the outlaws' pockets, which would insure a nice bust in town.

Walt Slade was not as carefree as the others, for he knew the chore assigned him was far from finished. He still had the outlaw bunch to deal with, and so far he had no idea who they were, where they hung out or, most important of all, who was the brains of the outfit. In fact, he had so far met no one whom he could consider a suspect.

Well, he hadn't been in the section long, and a good part of the time had been spent at Miguel Lopez' hacienda. Anyhow, he had made something of a start. The hellions had lost six of their number since he arrived in the Matagorda country. And he had pretty well dispelled the chimera of the men of steel who had terrorized the superstitious Mexicans and Texas-Mexicans of the section.

When they reached the point where the stretch of really rough water began, Slade again studied the rushing currents with interest. The tide was close to flood, and the waves were thundering on the jagged rocks and ledges. But again it seemed to him that the force of the water was much less than would have been expected. Again he turned to study the rises to the west. With the question that puzzled him unanswered, he rode on.

That night camp was made on a low mesa, from where

they could see for a considerable distance in every direction. The sky was brilliant with stars that cast a silvery sheen over the prairie. Nobody could approach the camp without being detected. Although he did not expect further trouble so soon, Slade was taking no chances—better to play it safe.

It wanted an hour of sunset, and they were only a few miles south of Port Lavaca, when he called the halt. But there was nothing to be gained by making a forced march that would bring them to town after dark.

"As it is, we'll make it in before noon tomorrow," he told Hernandez. "That will give you plenty of time to run the critters to Parr's corral and attend to the weighing and es-timate the wool cut. We'll get a good night's rest so the boys will be in shape for a mite of celebration tomorrow night. I figure they've earned it."

"Sure," agreed the range boss. "We are in no hurry. *Mañana!*"

The night passed quietly, and everybody enjoyed a good rest. The next day, before noon, the flock reached Port Lavaca and was safely corralled.

Eldon Parr did not appear particularly surprised at the arrival of the flock.

"Thought you'd get them through when I heard you rode south with Lopez," he said. "Glad to get them. A shipment from the east has been delayed for some reason or other—I don't know what. I'll pay off as soon as the estimates are in. Come back in two or three hours."

Meanwhile, the bodies of the men of steel were laid out for inspection in the sheriff's office. A long line of ex-cited citizens filed past to view them. Two were recognized as having hung around the saloons, but everybody was vague as to any associates they may have had.

"Ordinary border scum, the sort we are always getting here," said Sheriff Ross. "You can't tell what a jigger who rides in is—an honest cowhand or a chuck line rider or law-less hellion. Well, these are four good owlhoots now—the only sort that's any good, laid out stiff. Tin shirts and caps! Darn things do look like armor, at a glance, don't they? No wonder loco herders were fooled. And some gents who should know better weren't exactly easy in their minds," he added with a chuckle. "Do you think they'll pull out now that their masquerade has been uncovered?"

"They will not," Slade replied positively. "It's a smart and salty bunch and won't give up easily. From now on we can expect operations that are more orthodox, but just as deadly. Whoever had the brains and imagination to hit on that ruse to intimidate the herders will figure out some other devilish scheme. Very likely they'll start branching out now, too. There are things other than sheep productive of loot. Watch for something unexpected."

"I've been watching all the time, but I haven't been seeing," Ross returned morosely. "I've a notion, though, that you've got better 'eyes' than I have."

"More experience, rather," Slade replied. "What we want to do is, if possible, forestall anything they may have in mind. Otherwise somebody is very likely to die. They're killers and doubtless prefer to leave no witnesses. Well, let's go get something to eat, and then I'll accompany Hernandez to Parr's place to get paid off."

"What do you think of Parr's establishment?" the sheriff asked.

"Modern and efficient, from what little I saw of it," Slade replied. "I'd like to give it all a once-over; Parr appears to know his business."

"He does," agreed Ross. "No doubt as to that."

They repaired to the Post Hole and enjoyed a good meal. Hernandez joined them before they finished, and Slade waited for him to put away his surrounding. Then, together, they headed for Parr's packing house, where all was activity and orderly bustle.

Eldon Parr paid in cash, bills of large denominations, which Hernandez stowed in a buttoned pocket.

"Tell Lopez I can use another shipment, if he can manage to get it through," Parr said in parting.

"We'll get it through, all right," Hernandez declared. "And *gracias*, Mr. Parr."

As they walked along a quiet section of the street, where nobody was in sight, Slade felt the range boss thrust something into his hand.

"You take care of it," Hernandez said in low tones. "Too much money for me to be packing around. I want to get drunk in comfort tonight."

"Rather a large sum to entrust to El Halcón, don't you think?" Slade said as he pocketed the bills, his eyes dancing.

Hernandez' only answer was a smile.

"I'm heading for a cantina in the Mexican quarter over to the east," he announced a little later. "Know some folks over there. How about dropping around tonight? It's gay. Pretty *señoritas* on the dance floor, and they're nice. Liquor is good, and the games are straight. Called the Quetzal."

"Wouldn't be surprised if I do show up later," Slade answered. "Suppose all the boys will be there."

"Yes, it's their favorite hangout," Hernandez said. "Be seeing you."

Slade spent the remainder of the late afternoon sauntering about the town. He found it interesting, especially the waterfront, where several small ships were moored. Coastwise trading vessels, many of which, he well knew, dealt in contraband and were not above a little genteel smuggling. Their crew were a jolly, daredevil lot who were in the nature of seagoing cowhands, if such an anomaly could be imagined. Slade chuckled at the thought.

As dusk was falling, he saw a group of cowhands riding into town, one with a bandaged hand. At their head was Phil Waring, the owner of the W Diamond spread. He waved a greeting. Al Hodson held up his swathed member and grinned. Apparently he held no rancor for what had occurred in the Post Hole a few night before.

They were all in the Post Hole, at the bar, when Slade entered some time later in quest of something to eat. Waring spotted him at once and came over and dropped into a vacant chair.

"Feller, you sure been cutting a swath since you coiled your twine in this section," he chuckled. "You're the only jigger that's been able to make a stand against those blasted tin-shirted raiders. Keep up the good work and we'll all be in your debt. I lost cows myself last month. Didn't see any tin shirts, but I'm ready to swear it was the same bunch. What I'd like to know is where the devil do they run 'em. Not to the north or east, that's sure for certain, and I can't see them driving the critters across seventy miles of desert to the Rio Grande."

"Possibly load them on a ship that's put in and waiting," Slade replied.

"Uh-huh, that's what Ross figures, but I dunno," said Waring. "We trailed the herd for a while but lost the tracks on stony ground. Never could pick 'em up again. They were headed for the bay, all right, but we rode on to the shore and scouted it for miles below the bad water. Plenty of coves down there where a ship could put in, but we couldn't find a hoofprint anywhere. It had rained that night, and the ground and the sand were soft. Cows couldn't have passed that way without leaving tracks. They just didn't pass that way, that's all. But where in blazes did they go?"

"Sounds like something of a question," Slade conceded.

"That's why I was down that way the other day when you and Lopez met me," Waring continued. "I was having another look-see along the shore. Didn't find a thing. A few nights before, the Tolliver brothers, who own the M Cross T holding over to the west of my spread, lost a bunch of prime beef critters they were getting together for a shipping herd. *They* went somewhere, too, but where? Nobody seems able to come up with the answer. Maybe you can. You seem to be able to do anything."

"I fear you overestimate my ability," Slade smiled.

"I doubt it," Waring said. "Not after the way you shot a gun outa loco Al Hodson's hand before he could pull trigger and then sung everybody plumb peaceful. To say nothing of hypnotizing Mig Lopez' herders into running a flock to town, and downing four of the tin shirts in the bargain. I'm about ready to believe anything where you're concerned."

Suddenly he rocked with laughter. "Funny thing happened yesterday," he chuckled. "Al and me rode in to order some supplies. We stopped at the Occidental, down the street, for a drink. Got to talking to some fellers about you. A big blabbermouth who never was any good speaks up and says you are just a blasted owlhoot yourself. Al's right hand was tied up, but his left is pretty darn good. He wallops that jigger right on the nose with it, knocks him over a chair and to the floor. Then he picks up the chair and says, 'Another crack like that and I'll bust what's left of this chair over your skull, you terrapin-brained frazzle end of a misspent life!' Feller didn't say anything more."

They laughed together. "Guess I'll have to buy Al and the other boys a drink for that one," Slade said, beckoning a waiter.

"Much obliged," said Waring. "Al feels sorta beholden to you; if he'd done for Parr, he would have been in trouble, just as Ross said. "Hot-tempered hellion, but he's a real *amigo* if he happens to cotton to you. Here comes Frog-lip Fogarty with a drink. He sorta cottons to you, too. He likes good music, and him and Miguel Lopez are chummy."

Frog-lip placed the glasses on the table, very tenderly. "From my private bottle," he announced.

"Uh-huh, I remember that private bottle," said Waring. "An innocent stranger who smelled the cork was crippled for life. Well, I've lived a good life. Here goes!"

He downed the drink at a gulp, smacked his lips and winked at Slade. The Ranger sipped his and concluded that

Frog-lip was a connoisseur of good whiskey. His meal arrived at that moment, and he proceeded to do it full justice, while Waring smoked and talked.

"Reckon Parr was glad to get that flock, wasn't he?" he suddenly remarked.

"He appeared pleased," Slade replied.

"An ornery hellion, but he knows his business," Waring said. "Understand he's making money hand over fist. But if he tries to run sheep onto the open range hereabouts, he's in for trouble. Sheep spoil range."

"Not if they're handled properly, as you very well know," Slade countered.

"Uh-huh, but what guarantee do we have that a rapscallion like Parr will handle them properly?" Waring retorted. "He's just the sort that would let 'em eat the grass down to nothing and the devil with it."

"Why don't you people get title to the land?" Slade asked. "It would pay you to do so."

"Takes money, for one thing," Waring answered. "The state don't let this good grassland go cheap. Besides, most of the owners hereabouts are old fellers who have been here all their lives, and their dads before them. They've always looked on the range as part of their holdings. Use it to handle their overflow, and there's never been any friction. They figure why should they pay out good money for what is rightfully theirs by occupancy."

Slade was silent. It was the old argument advanced by the barons of the open range, used against the advancing farmers and sheepmen. They always lost in the end, but all too often not without bloodshed. It could happen here. This was another disturbing angle to the problem that confronted him.

His thoughts turned to the vanished cows. He was definitely inclined to go along with Waring's opinion that they could not be driven across the desert to the distant Rio Grande and a ready market south of the border. The cattle of the section were not obstreperous longhorns, heavily wiry, but improved stock—docile, slow-moving, heavily fleshed. They were easy to round up and drive, but no good where rough going prevailed and speed was essential. But where the devil did they go! Although evidence appeared to the contrary, Slade rather believed that Waring might have overlooked some obscure cove or inlet where a ship could put in to receive them.

Waring was still making derogatory remarks anent Eldon

Parr. Slade began to wonder slightly if he was doing so with the purpose of instilling prejudice against the packer. It was not beyond the realm of possibility. If so, what was his objective? Another interesting angle to ponder.

However, Waring's final observation did not tend to confirm the suspicion.

"I suppose I shouldn't be sounding off about the hellion as I have been, just because he made me mad and I don't like him," he said. "After all, I've never known him to do anything off-color, nor has anybody else, so far as I've heard. And I've a notion his threat to run in sheep is, the chances are, just making big medicine. He's uppity and bad tempered, but you can't blame a jigger too much for how he's made. Al Hodson is a fine feller, but plumb loco if he happens to get his mad up. No more judgment than a Comanche buck full of hooch. And I reckon I ain't a plumb perfect bargain myself."

His crooked but very white teeth flashed in a grin as he spoke. His expression became speculative, and he asked a question.

"Figure to stick around the section for a while?"

"For a while," Slade admitted.

Waring nodded. "Then if you happen to be looking for a chore of riding, how about signing up with me?" he asked. "I've been handling the range boss chores myself since Tim Potter died a few months back, and I've got plenty to do without that. How about it?"

Slade considered for a moment; the offer was not without attraction. It would give him a legitimate excuse for remaining in the section, and he had a feeling that somehow the W Diamond might be the focus of activity in the future.

"I'm riding back to Miguel Lopez' place with his boys, tomorrow, but I'll think on it," he promised. "However, I'll make one stipulation if I do decide to sign on with you. I am to handle things as I think they should be handled, without interference from anybody, subject only to the check of the owner."

"Well, I don't think any of the boys will argue with you, after what happened in here the other night," Waring said dryly. "Not even Al Hodson is that loco. Okay, we'll let it stand as is till you make up your mind. Now I guess I'd better amble over to the bar and see how the boys are making out. Best to keep an eye on 'em when the snorts get to buzzin' in their ears. Be seeing you."

He strode off, swaggering a little, apparently his habitual

gait. Slade smiled as he watched him go. He finished his dinner, enjoyed a cigarette over a final cup of coffee, steaming hot, and pondered what should be his next move. Recalling that he had tentatively promised Hernandez that he would visit him at the cantina, the Quetzal, he decided it wouldn't be a bad notion. He was getting a bit weary of the uproar in the Post Hole, which apparently was noted for noise. A stroll in the cool night air wouldn't go bad.

It was pleasant under the stars after the hullabaloo he had just left, and he strolled along at a leisurely pace. As he worked his way east, the streets grew quieter and darker. Having a pretty good idea where the cantina was located, he turned a corner, walked south a block and turned another corner. And barged smack into a shindig.

9

‡❮❮❮❮❮❮❮❮❮❮❮❮❮❮❮❮❮❮❮❮❮❮❮❮❮❮❮❮❮❯

AT THE MOUTH of an alley, a few yards distant, two men were wrestling furiously. Slade instantly recognized one as Sebastian Hernandez, the Lopez range boss. A third man dodged about, trying to get behind Hernandez, a knife raised to strike.

Slade bounded forward, caught the descending wrist just in time. He gave it a terrific wrench. There was a snapping sound, the knife tinkled to the ground and the wielder gave a yelp of pain. Slade hit with his left hand, grazed the other's jaw, but with enough force to knock him off his feet; he scuttled into the alley on all fours, and his racing steps sounded back from the darkness. The other man tore free from Hernandez, tripping the range boss, who fell heavily, and fled into the alley after his companion. Slade half drew his guns, then thought better of it. He didn't know what the score was, and a killing might not be justified. Could be a private row over a *señorita*, or something. A moment later he was to regret his indecision.

Hernandez, all the breath knocked out of him, was scrambling to his feet. He gave a strangled yell.

"Shoot them! Shoot the *ladrones!*"

"Hold it," Slade told him. "They're gone. What is this all about?"

"They were after the money, the blankety-blank-blanks!" Hernandez gasped, trying to pump some wind into his lungs. "They knew right where to look for it, the mangy horned toads!"

"Simmer down and tell me what happened," Slade said. "I can't make head or tail of your gabble."

Hernandez grew quieter as his breath returned. "I was heading for the Post Hole from the cantina right down the street, to look for you," he explained. "As I passed that alley, the two hellions closed in on me from behind. One jabbed a knife into my ribs and said, 'Elevate!' With that sticker against my back I didn't argue. The other one reached right for my inside pocket and began unbuttoning it. That made me good and mad. The one with the knife had eased back a trifle, so I took a chance and slid sideways from it—grained the skin a little—and grabbed the other one by the neck. I'd pretty near got to my gun when you showed up. Lucky for me you did; I'd have gotten that blade in my back if you hadn't. Guess that's all."

"And plenty," Slade said. "Yes, I missed a trick by not blasting the sidewinders. You all right? Did he cut you much?"

"Oh, just a scratch," Hernandez said. "Sorta spoiled my coat, though, I'm afraid." He turned to show a long tear in the back of the garment.

"Come on back to the cantina where we can get a look at it," Slade said. "A sharp knife doesn't pain much, and you might be hurt more than you think. Doesn't appear to be bleeding much, but best not to take chances."

"Okay," agreed Hernandez. "Right down the street a couple of blocks, where you see the light."

They headed for the cantina, Hernandez walking without difficulty. Slade did not think he was seriously injured but wanted to make sure.

The Quetzal was big, softly lighted and much quieter than the Post Hole. A really good orchestra provided music, and the *señoritas* of the dance floor were all Hernandez had claimed for them.

The proprietor, plump and jolly and efficient-looking, came hurrying forward to greet them.

"Back so soon, Sebastian?" he exclaimed. "I am glad you found your *amigo* so quickly. Welcome, *Capitán!* My humble establishment is indeed honored. It is the great pleasure to be host to El Halcón."

His smile changed to a look of concern when Hernandez told him what had happened, and he led the way to a back room where the range boss stripped off coat and shirt, baring his sinewy back.

Slade was relieved to find that the wound was really very slight. Some salve and a few strips of plaster, which the owner produced from a drawer, took care of it.

"And now," said Hernandez as he donned his garments, "now I feel the need of a drink, two drinks, a whole flock of drinks. Getting knifed always makes me thirsty."

"I think I'll settle for coffee," Slade decided.

The proprietor escorted them to a table, seated them with a flourish and cared for their order himself.

"On the house," he said. "I will have it no other way. I repeat, I am honored." With a bow and a smile, he left to attend to various chores.

" 'Pears to be a right hombre," Slade commented.

"He is," said Hernandez. "They don't come any better."

Hernandez sipped his wine in silence for a while. "Wonder how the devil those hellions knew just where to look for that money?" he suddenly remarked. "Somebody must have watched me stow it away and tipped them off."

"Looks that way," Slade agreed noncommittally; he was wondering about it himself.

"Knew I was doing the right thing when I gave it to you to carry," Hernandez said, with a chuckle.

"Well, the way it turned out, there would have been no harm if you'd been packing it," Slade replied.

"Maybe," the range boss conceded dubiously. "Just the same, I'm glad you have it and not me. Guess that pair will have something to remember you by. I'm pretty sure you busted the arm of the one with the knife. Sure sounded like it, the way he yelped. Wonder if he'll go to Doc Price to have it set?"

Slade shook his head. "Not likely," he replied. "Whoever sent them to do the chore would be too smart for that. He'll have it attended to elsewhere."

"Wouldn't be surprised if you're right," Hernandez conceded. "I didn't get much of a look at him, but I think I'd recognize the other *ladrón* if I see him. Hope so; I'll give him more than a busted arm if I do. Oh, the devil with 'em! Let's enjoy ourselves."

Slade did enjoy his visit to the Quetzal. He had several dances with the *señoritas*, who proved as charming as they were pretty, yielded to a request to sing. His offering was greeted with thunderous applause, and several encores were demanded. After a while, however, he glanced at the clock over the bar.

"Guess you'd better round up your boys and call it a night," he told Hernandez. "We want to get a fairly early start back to the ranch, and it's late."

The range boss cheerfully acquiesced, and a little later they left the cantina in a body.

"Now let the sidewinders try something!" Hernandez growled. "We'll make chili stew of them."

However, the outlaws failed to oblige, which under the circumstances was not surprising.

The following morning, Slade paused at the sheriff's office before heading back to Lopez' spread and acquainted Ross with what had happened the night before.

"So the hellions have started operating in town," snorted the peace officer. "My troubles are getting no better fast. You be back soon?"

"In a day or two," Slade replied. "Be seeing you."

When they reached the bad water south of town, Slade once more slowed up and surveyed the bay. On former occasions, the tide had been at flood. Now it was at ebb, and although the waves still swirled and eddied and pounded the rocks, the current which had so intrigued him was practically non-existent. His black brows drew together until the concentration furrow was deep between them, a sure sign that El Halcón was doing some hard thinking. He turned to gaze northward, shook his head and rode on.

With nothing untoward happening, they arrived at the hacienda as the sun was setting in amber and gold. They were warmly welcomed by *Don* Miguel, who swore in several languages when Hernandez regaled him with a graphic account of routing of the wide-loopers and the frustration of the robbery attempt. When the range boss paused, he solemnly shook hands with Slade.

"And that should settle the blasted men of steel," he said. "I'll spread the word around among the other flock owners. Maybe we'll have peace now."

Slade shook his head. "I doubt it," he differed. "I'm of the opinion they'll give up their bizarre masquerade, now that it's been uncovered, and they haven't much choice but to do so. But they won't stop operating—not so long as the business is profitable, as it undoubtedly is. A smart and salty owlhoot outfit doesn't give up just because of a setback. They'll break loose again, perhaps where, when and how least expected."

"Here?" *Don* Miguel asked.

"Not likely, I'd say," Slade replied. "They'll know you are very much on the alert and that your boys are spoiling for another whack at them. I think they'll fight shy of your Tumbling L spread, at least for a while. They might make a try if they figure you've been lulled into a false sense of security. Your excellent stock is a temptation to any outlaw bunch, and you're strategically situated, from their point of view, not far from the bay and near where there are many little coves and inlets. That is, if they do run the stolen sheep and cattle onto a waiting ship, which it seems logical to believe. Yes, they might give it a whirl if they figure you've gotten careless."

"I won't get careless," Lopez promised grimly. "I'm on the lookout for anything so long as the hellions are still in existence, which I've a notion they won't be for long, not with El Halcón on their trail."

"Hope you're right," Slade said, "but at present they are still very much in existence, and I predict they won't wait long to pull something. When an outlaw leader suffers a reverse, he has to get busy and make a haul to bolster the morale of his followers."

Walt Slade quickly proved himself no mean prophet. The next day, in midafternoon, Manuel Garcia, *Don* Miguel's neighbor to the west, rode up to the Tumbling L casa in anything but a good temper.

"I lost a hundred head last night," he explained. "Just vanished into the clouds, or so my herders swear."

"Well, they didn't," Lopez said flatly. "Haven't been to town for a few days, have you, Manuel?" Garcia shook his head.

"If you had, you'd have heard what I'm going to tell you," Lopez continued. There followed a pungently profane account of the unmasking of the men of steel and the killing of six of their number. Garcia said things he never learned in the Mission school.

"I knew all along it was just some sort of skullduggery, but try and make my herders believe it," he concluded. "Now maybe they will believe me."

"I'd planned to send Hernandez and a couple of the boys to talk to them tomorrow," Lopez said. "And we'll spread the word to Telo and Ybarra and the others. Men of steel! Just a bunch of owlhoots in tin shirts! Doesn't seem possible anybody *would* believe such nonsense."

"Well, when we were children, we believed in fairies and St. Nick, and that the Devil went about in horns and a tail, gnashing his teeth, and unfortunately most of the herders and the *peones* of the river villages have never gotten beyond the childhood stage," Garcia pointed out. "The legend of the men of steel has come down from father to son, and the story never lost anything in the telling. But the rest of them, like your boys, will be good and mad at being made fools of. This business has got to be stopped, Miguel. We've all got to work together, and with Mr. Slade here to handle things as they should be handled, I have little doubt as to the final outcome."

"Agreed," said Lopez. "Come on, it's time to eat. You might as well spend the night and head back to your place in the morning. I'll have Hernandez and a couple of the boys ride with you."

"And I'll ride with you also, if you don't mind," Slade said. "I'd like to have a look at the pasture from which your woollies were wide-looped."

"*Gracias*, Mr. Slade, that is fine of you," Garcia instantly responded. "The presence of El Halcón will do much to allay my herders' fears."

10

AFTER A TWO-HOUR RIDE through a morning of sparkling sunshine, Slade and Garcia, accompanied by Hernandez and two of the Tumbling L herders, reached the Garcia casa. The owner at once dispatched messengers to order his herders to assemble at the ranchhouse before sundown. This chore attended to, he and Slade had a cup of coffee and then headed for the pasture from which the sheep had been purloined.

"I've a notion it might be possible to trail them," Slade explained.

"I doubt it," Garcia replied. "The grass is very heavy and springs up almost immediately after it is trod down."

Slade nodded but did not otherwise comment. When they arrived at the pasture, he dismounted and carefully scanned the ground. After a while, he motioned Garcia to join him.

"Look close," he said. "See these two grass blades, the heads of which have been broken and are dangling against the stem. You'll notice the break is not very recent; the ends have begun to brown."

Garcia squatted and peered where Slade designated. "Yes," he said, "now that I'm right up against it I can see the break. How you did while standing up is beyond me, but then most things El Halcón does are beyond the average individual. And what meaning do you read into it?"

"A horse's iron not only treads the grass down, it sometimes cuts the stems," Slade explained. "That's what happened here. If a sheep's hoof cut it, the break will be slanting and blurred. You will notice these cuts are straight across the stem, which means that horses were here. Your herders are not mounted, I take it."

"That's right," Garcia admitted.

"So the horse that left this track was ridden by one of the wide-loopers," Slade said. "Now all we have to do is follow the trail left by the horses, and we'll get an idea where your sheep went. Simple, is it not?"

"For one with your eyes," grunted the other. "For an individual with average good eyesight, like myself, not at all simple. In fact, impossible."

Slade smiled and resumed his examination of the ground.

"Here they go," he said at length, "headed almost due east. I've a notion they'll turn toward the bay a little later."

They didn't. Mile after mile Slade was able to follow the trail, by slow going. On places where the grass was sparse, the task was not difficult for the Ranger, but when the heavier growth renewed, only the most painstaking examination revealed the slight traces of the flock's passage.

The wind, blowing from the south had been steadily increasing in force, until it was almost of gale proportions, tossing the manes of the horses, bending the grass. Although it buffeted the riders, it tempered the heat of the sun, which was an advantage.

They had covered many miles when, quite a distance ahead, appeared a wide stretch of sandy ground that was desert-like. Over it a wavering mist seemed to hang. Slade uttered an exclamation of exasperation.

"What's the matter?" Garcia asked.

Slade gestured ahead. "See what looks like a thin fog over the sand?" he said. "This hard wind is shifting the sand. By the time we get there, all tracks left by horses and sheep will be filled in and obliterated. Trail's end, so far as we're concerned. No telling which way they may have turned."

For some moments he was silent, his brows drawing together. Garcia watched him expectantly. At the edge of the desert strip, which he knew extended for many miles, he pulled Shadow to a halt.

The sands *were* moving. Soon they would be flying in blinding clouds. Slade shook his head, turned and gazed south.

"We'll ride down to the bay," he decided. "We'll follow the shoreline for a while and see if we can spot anything." He glanced at the westering sun.

"Don't mind getting in late?" he asked.

"I'll stay out all night if you say the word," Garcia replied.

"Won't be that bad," Slade said. "And you can spend the night at Lopez' place. Hernandez and his boys are talking to your herders, so there's no real reason we have to be back at your spread tonight. And I do want to have a look at that shoreline."

"Okay by me," Garcia acquiesced cheerfully. "Let's go."

Turning due south, they rode until they were close to the water's edge, where Slade again turned east, walking his horse, scanning the soft earth and the damp sands. From time to time he shook his head, but he said nothing until they had passed the mesa where the row with the men of steel had occurred and reached the beginning of the turbulent water, where the waves were pounding the rocks, the eddies swirling.

"Got me beat," Slade said, halting Shadow. "It doesn't seem credible that they would continue east past the bad water and then turn south. They'd be dangerously close to town. A ship putting in would quite likely be spotted. And it takes time to load stock onto one of those small coastline vessels. But if they didn't where the devil did they go? The tracks led to the edge of the desert and presumably continued in the same direction. Well, we've done all we can today. Almost sunset. Let's head for home."

It was well past dark when they reached the Lopez ranchhouse. Despite his loss of the night before, Garcia was in a cheerful mood.

"I feel confident I won't have any more trouble with my herders," he said. "And with them properly on the job, I won't suffer any more losses."

"I've a notion you're right," Slade agreed. "Well, we should hear something."

They did. Hernandez was in the living room with *Don* Miguel when they entered.

"Was getting a mite worried about you," Lopez said. "Glad to see you both back okay."

Garcia glanced expectantly at Hernandez, who chuckled.

"They're boiling mad," he said, apropos of Garcia's herders. "They don't take kindly to having been made fools of. Any men of steel who come snooping around had better be wearing boiler plate from now on, or something that'll stop .45 slugs. The boys are itching for a chance at them. Two of them rode to visit Telo and the others and spread the word around. They say that with El Halcón here, men of steel or no men of steel, there's nothing to worry about."

"That's fine," Slade smiled, "but they and the rest of you must remember that you've still got a dangerous outlaw bunch to contend with. So don't become overconfident."

He acquainted *Don* Miguel with the results, or rather the lack of results of their long day's ride.

"Anyhow, we proved rather conclusively that they didn't go up into the clouds," he concluded. "They stuck close to the ground for so far as we were able to follow them, and I think they continued to stick to it until they took to the water in some manner. Well, we'll try and learn how that was done."

"There's the cook bellerin' for you fellers to come and get it," said Lopez. "He insisted on waiting up for you. Said he would be dishonored if he allowed El Halcón to go hungry." He led the way to the dining room, where Slade thanked the cook for his consideration, speaking in courteous Spanish that left the old fellow beaming.

After eating, Slade walked out for a look at the weather. It had all the appearances of another wild night. The wind had increased in violence, and the sky was black as ink.

He wasn't surprised, however, for the season of Gulf storms was at hand. He went to bed, dismissed all his problems and slept soundly.

Toward morning the storm blew itself out, after a drenching rain, and when Slade arose, the sky was clear, the wind greatly abated. He enjoyed a leisurely breakfast and sat with Lopez in the living room, smoking and talking. The owner suggested that he look things over, which they proceeded to do. Slade was impressed by the excellent condition of everything. The ranchhouse, built in the Spanish style with an inner patio, was old but in perfect repair. The same went for the bunkhouses, barn and other buildings.

"I've always been proud of my holding, which I inherited from my father," Lopez said. "I would never allow it to get rundown. It is all I have to look after, aside from numerous poor relations, as I mentioned once before. I am a bachelor, no chick or child. When I pass on, the place will go to Hernandez and the others. So I consider myself in the nature of a trustee for those who come after me."

"A truly laudable viewpoint," Slade replied. "But I trust it will be a long time before you slack off your hold on the twine. You're good for forty years yet."

"I hope so," Lopez chuckled. "I find life interesting, but no doubt the hereafter will also be interesting. I think I will last for a while, though, that is if the outlaws will just give me a little peace, That, however, I am confident is on the way. As the herders say, now that El Halcón is here, there is nothing to worry about."

Shortly before noon, an excited *vaquero* who rode for Alfredo Telo paused at the ranchhouse.

"A ship was wrecked over where the bad water begins," he reported. "She is partly sunken and wedged between two reefs close to the shore. The crew, I fear, are lost, for I saw nobody on or near the vessel. She must have been driven ashore by last night's storm."

Don Miguel uttered a horrified exclamation.

Slade asked, "Is she breaking up?"

The *vaquero* shook his head. "Not yet," he replied, "but when the tide turns, doubtless she will, or if the wind rises again."

Slade turned to Lopez. "Suppose we ride over there for a look," he suggested. "Might be possible to do something for somebody. Strange that no survivors were seen, for she must have struck close to the shore."

"Let us go," said Lopez.

They quickly got the rigs on their horses and rode east at a fast pace.

"I never knew such a thing to happen before," said Lopez. "On stormy nights, the beacons are always lighted to guide vessels to the safety of the channel beyond the bad water. No ship puts in close to shore until the beacon is seen. They stand well off the dangerous coast and do not attempt to draw near until the signal beckons them. Then they steer for it, knowing it the harbinger of safety."

"Always the chance of human error," Slade replied. "Skipper might have been unfamiliar with the coast and become confused. Perhaps we will be able to learn just what happened."

In due time they sighted the vessel. As the *vaquero* had said, she was firmly wedged between two reefs and, with the tide out, was quite close to shore. There was a great hole in the bow, at and below the water line, but otherwise she looked stanch enough, and Slade was of the opinion that it would be some time before she broke up.

She was a small schooner of the kind often seen along the Gulf Coast. The fore topmast was broken off at the fids and lay, a welter of cordage and canvas, across the deck. The mainmast still stood but appeared wobbly.

Opposite the wreck they pulled to a halt and sat gazing at the battered schooner. There was no sign of life aboard.

"Strange!" Slade suddenly exclaimed. *Don* Miguel glanced at him questioningly.

"She is fitted for two lifeboats, and they're both still in the davits," Slade explained. "That really is strange. When the order to abandon ship came, as it surely must have when she struck, what did the crew do—jump overboard?"

"Hmmm! Does look funny," conceded Lopez. "Think they're still aboard? Maybe asleep?"

"They'd hardly be asleep under such circumstances," Slade replied, with a smile.

"Maybe knocked unconscious when she struck and still out," hazarded Lopez.

"That is also unlikely," Slade answered. He measured the distance to the vessel's side with his eyes.

"*Don* Miguel," he said, "the water is not too deep for the horses to wade, and strange to say, there is a wide strip of placid water beyond the bow. I believe at the bow, which is very low in the water, we can stand in the saddles and get aboard. I'd like to have a look around."

They put the horses to the water, and when they reached the ship's side, it was not much more than belly-deep on the animals. Slade stood in the saddle and managed to get a grip on the rail. He swung himself onto the slanting deck, reached down and gave Lopez a hand. In a moment the other was standing beside him.

"Captain's cabin should be aft," Slade said, glancing around the deserted deck. "Let's have a look at that first."

Without difficulty they reached the cabin, descended two steps and found the floor awash with a foot of water. It was a typical mariner's abode—chairs and a table bolted to the floor, a wide bunk, sea chest and other furnishings. The water was dotted with papers half-submerged, soaked and blurred. In one corner, bolted to deck and bulkhead, was a big iron safe. The door stood open, and a glance showed Slade that the combination knob had been knocked off, presumably with a sledgehammer.

"Now what the devil?" he muttered, staring at the damaged strongbox, which to all appearances had been rifled of its contents.

"Looks like somebody other than the captain opened that safe," *Don* Miguel observed dryly.

"Yes, it certainly does," Slade agreed. "Now what's the answer to this one?"

"Perhaps the crew mutinied, killed and robbed the captain and abandoned ship," Lopez hazarded.

"Possibly," Slade conceded, without comment.

"Me-ee-ow!" sounded plaintively from across the cabin.

11

SLADE TURNED, staring. On the bunk, which was clear of the water, stood a cat, a very disgusted looking cat who apparently was not at all intrigued with the position in which it found itself. Slade sloshed across to the bunk and rubbed its ears. The cat purred happily, arched its back and butted its head against his palm.

"Here's another queer one," he said. "Sailors are almost universally very superstitious about the ship's cat, almost as superstitious as herders where 'men of steel' are concerned. They would be loath to abandon one, feeling that the act would surely bring them bad luck. The most callous deepwater man would hesitate to do so. Yet here we find this little critter by itself on a deserted ship. If the sailors swam or waded ashore —they assuredly didn't use the boats—they would almost certainly have taken their cat with them. And—blast it!—I still keep wondering why the ship would put in to shore close enough to be caught by one of those currents and hurled onto the rocks. The whole affair just doesn't make sense."

"Perhaps it's the ship that's been packing off the stolen sheep and cattle—it figured to put in at a cove and somehow missed its bearings," Lopez guessed.

Slade shook his head. "I thought of that and gave her sides a careful once-over as we rode up to her," he replied. "There are no indications of a hinged section that could be let down to form a loading gangplank for sheep or cows. Here, you look after the cat and I'll try and salvage some of those papers floating around—might learn something from them."

Lopez sat down on the bunk, drew his feet up out of the water and cuddled the cat, which appeared much better satisfied now that it had human company. Slade fished papers out of the water, groping for those that had sunk, and studied the almost illegible writing.

"I've got part of her manifest," he said at length. " 'Pears her cargo is, or was, hides and tallow. But I'll wager she was packing something else in that safe, something more compact and more valuable."

"Money?" asked Lopez.

"Quite likely, or its equivalent in some form," Slade agreed. "Anyhow, something valuable enough to induce somebody to smash open that safe and clean it, tossing papers and everything else aside until they located what they were after."

Outside sounded a loud whinny. Slade raised his head.

"It's Shadow telling us the tide's turned and the water's rising," he said. "Come on, we've got to get out of here. I want a quick look into the forecastle before we leave."

He scooped up the cat and led the way to the outside and down the slanting deck to the crew's quarters beyond the foremast, in which the water was deeper. He took a quick, all-embracing glance around, paused a moment, then returned to where Lopez waited.

"Another funny one," he said. "In there are eleven duffel-bags, the packs in which sailors carry their belongings. They are neatly stacked in place and not opened. If possible, a sailor would take his duffelbag along, or at least open it to remove something of particular value. Eleven bags. Eleven would be a reasonable number of crewmen for a ship this size. Things are getting more loco all the time. Come on, let's go."

Cradling the cat in one arm, he let himself down over the rail, teetered on the hull for a moment and slid down, gripping Shadow's barrel with his legs, until his feet were in the stirrups. He reached up to help Lopez descend. Together they headed for the shore, the horses snorting their disgust, for the water was now almost up to their withers.

On the shore, Slade drew rein and sat gazing back at the ship for a moment, then turned his head to glance west.

"Now what?" asked Lopez.

"I just thought of something," Slade replied, shifting the cat to a more comfortable position. "I want to have a look at the mesa a mile or so back, where we had the wring with the men of steel."

Upon reaching the mesa, Slade slowed Shadow to a walk. Abruptly, near the east slope, he drew rein and sat staring at a wide blackened spot formed by a huge heap of ashes and partly burned tree branches. He gave a low whistle.

"I thought so," he said. "*Don* Miguel, we're heading for town and the sheriff."

"Why?" asked the mystified Lopez.

"Because we have something to report to him," Slade said slowly. "*Don* Miguel—"

"Oh, blast it, stop *Don*-ing me," Lopez exclaimed impatiently. "Call me Mig, like all my friends do. Now what were you going to say?"

"All right, Mig," Slade smiled, although he was in no mood for mirth. "That ship did not mistakenly get off its course and get caught by the currents. It was deliberately wrecked."

"Wrecked!" exclaimed Lopez. "How do you know?"

"The night I had my first wring with the men of steel, when I downed a pair of them and got my head nicked, I saw a big heap of twigs and dry branches and other fuel," Slade replied. "I wondered what it was for but concluded that the bunch planned to make a fire and cook. I was wrong. That night I also saw a ship standing well off shore. And I saw the beacon flare atop a rise far to the east, the beacon that was to guide the ship to the safety of the channel. That night the devils planned to light a false beacon down here this side of the bad water and far from the safe channel. The fire here was intended to lure the ship in closer to the shore, where those vicious currents would catch her and slam her on the rocks. Because I downed the pair who were to handle the chore, the fire wasn't lighted and the ship was saved. Last night was a different story. Last night the false beacon was lighted, the ship moved in closer, expecting to find the channel, and was wrecked. Why? That remains to be learned. Robbery of some sort, of course. Somebody knew the "Compostella"—that was the name I read on the manifest papers, I believe—was packing something of value, money or something else. So they wrecked her and, I'm very much afraid, murdered the captain and the crew and cast their bodies into the water, where the outgoing tide would carry them away. Understand now?"

"Yes, I reckon I do," Lopez said, with a shudder. "The snake-blooded scoundrels."

"They're all of that," Slade agreed. "I'm beginning to remember things now. I recall one of the second bunch that came along after I'd regained consciousness saying, 'No wonder there wasn't any blaze.' And another said, 'A nice haul gone to the devil!' I had no notion what they meant, then, but now I understand it. I told Sheriff Ross that they would very likely be branching out. Well, they are, with a vengeance, in a way I did not suspect. All right, cat, get comfortable. You've got a long ride ahead of you. Yes, I know you're hungry. So am I. But we'll have to wait till we get to town to put on the nosebag. That is, unless you'd care to nibble a little grass. No? Okay, you'll have to make the best of it for a while."

He snuggled the furry mariner against his breast, where it promptly went to sleep.

It was well past dark when they reached Port Lavaca. First they paused at the Post Hole to turn the cat over to Frog-lip Fogarty, who took it to the kitchen for a surroundin'. Then they cared for their horses and went in search of the sheriff.

They found him in his office, just about ready to close up shop for the day. Slade gave him an account of the wreck and what he suspected.

"Try and find out what you can about that ship," he concluded. "Having her name, you should be able to glean some information relative to her registry, where she sailed from and so forth."

"Ah, Lord!" groaned the sheriff. "Sooner or later I will have to grow fins. Say, what you grinning about? I don't see anything funny."

"I was thinking," Slade said with a chuckle, "that it's fortunate I'm not superstitious, like the herders. Otherwise I'd be inclined to believe somebody did come down from the clouds and went back up into them."

"Now what the devil do you mean by that?" Ross demanded irritably.

"Just this," Slade replied. "The ground down there is very soft for quite a distance in every direction, we had a heavy rain last night, and yet there wasn't a hoofprint, a boot print, or any other kind of a print anywhere in the vicinity of where the ship was grounded. Nobody approached the wreck from the shore, or left it by way of the shore, either."

"By the water, then," growled the sheriff.

"So it would seem," Slade conceded. "But to all appearances it would be impossible for a boat to live in that maelstrom. So unless there is some condition there that I so far have been unable to fathom, that is a very unsatisfactory answer, and no real solution of the mystery."

"Oh, the devil!" snorted Ross. "Let's go get something to eat and a drink or two; I need both."

At the Post Hole they found that Frog-lip had already fallen in love with the cat.

"Fine little beast," he declared. "Ate a pound of chopped beef, drank a saucer of milk and scratched the cook on the ankle. Then went to sleep on a sack of oats. He's got a home."

"Well, looks like we accomplished something," chuckled Lopez. "Another poor relation to be looked after. I'll pay for his keep, Frog-lip."

"Ain't a boarder," said Frog-lip. "Didn't I tell you he's got a home!"

"So that load's off my shoulders," Lopez said, with a grin. "Better take out adoption papers, Frog-lip, so everything will be legal. All right, send us a waiter; we're all three as hungry as the cat was."

"And I'll send over a drink, on the cat," said Frog-lip. He ambled off.

The food soon arrived, and the hungry men got busy, with very little conversation until final cups of coffee were brought and they relaxed in full-fed comfort with cigarettes.

"There's Doc Price and Eldon Parr!" Ross suddenly exclaimed. He waved and beckoned.

Price and Parr turned and approached the table. A waiter brought extra chairs, and they sat down.

"How are you, Mr. Slade, any new adventures since I last saw you?" Parr asked.

Ross immediately broke in with an account of the wreck. Parr listened intently and shook his big head.

"Lamentable," he said. "It seems that a wave of lawlessness is sweeping the deestrict. Things used to be quite peaceable."

Walt Slade's eyes narrowed the merest trifle, but his only comment was a nod.

"Let a blasted owlhoot bunch move into a section, and all hell busts loose," growled the sheriff. "There won't be any more peace till the hellions eat lead or stretch rope."

"Well, some of them have eaten lead, thanks to Walt," said Lopez. "If he'll just stick around with us, I've a notion the whole bunch will be cleaned out before long. By the way, Walt, riding back to my place with me in the morning?"

"I think I'll ride over to Phil Waring's spread in the morning," Slade replied. "I promised him I would. Expect to head for your place day after tomorrow, though. I'm curious about that ship, and Neale may learn something relative to her tomorrow, so I might as well stick around here another day. I'll be back from Waring's holding by dark. I understand it's only a couple of hours' ride to his casa."

"That's right," said Ross. "Just follow the northwest trail and you can't miss it—runs right past his house."

Eldon Parr's expression did not change when Phil Waring's name was mentioned, but Slade thought the hard glitter in the pale depths of his eyes intensified.

The conversation drifted into other channels, and general range matters were discussed for a while. Eldon Parr beckoned a waiter and ordered a round of drinks. He emptied his glass and stood up.

"Have to be leaving you, gentlemen," he said. "A busy day ahead of me tomorrow. Got a shipment of woollies in today, from my place over east." With a nod he left the saloon.

"Neale, do you happen to know where Parr originated?" Slade asked.

"Born and brought up in east Texas, Neches River country, I believe he said," Ross replied. "Talks sort of educated, don't you think?"

"He does," Slade said briefly.

Doc Price glanced at the clock. "I'm going, too," he said. "Stay at my place tonight, Walt?"

"Be glad to," Slade accepted. "I'm ready for bed. Be seeing you in a day or two, Mig. I'll drop in at the office late tomorrow, Neale, and find out if you've learned anything."

12

==

BEING QUITE WEARY after the day's hectic events, Slade slept rather late. It was midmorning when he got the rig on Shadow and headed for Phil Waring's place, riding north by west. After a while he turned and gazed back at the huddle of buildings on the low bluff. With an engineer's knowledge of geological formations and the peculiarities of tides and currents, he knew that so far as its present status was concerned, the port town was doomed. Slowly but surely the tides and currents were choking the channel and destroying the deepwater facilities. The whole coastline would change. Where were now dangerous reefs and shoals would be placid water, and vice versa. Later, land developments would very probably restore the town to its former prosperity, but that would be some time in the future. He rode on, pondering the inscrutable eccentricities of the sea.

Soon he was passing over excellent pasture. Here, he knew, was open range, so called—state lands which the cowmen of the section looked upon as their own. For an hour and slightly more he continued until he knew that, according to what Sheriff Ross had told him, he was on Phil Waring's W Diamond holding. Now there was a range of low rises to the north, some six or seven hundred yards distant. They were heavily brush-grown with what appeared to be a gradual trend to the northwest. And directly ahead he sighted a singular equipage.

It was a big freight wagon loaded high with provisions and other articles. There was nothing strange about a wagon being on the trail, but this one looked out of the ordinary. It was tilted askew—that gave it a lopsided appearance.

"Right rear wheel came off," Slade remarked to Shadow. "Fellows are trying to get it back on and not having any luck."

Two figures were working over the axle. One was tall and bulky, the other slender, not very tall and slightly built, dressed in overalls, soft blue shirt and broad-brimmed "J.B." set at a jaunty angle. And as Slade drew nearer he saw red-gold curly hair under the hatbrim; the smaller of the pair was a girl.

A moment later he recognized the man to be Al Hodson, the rider for Waring who had had the row with Eldon Parr.

The recognition was mutual. Hodson let out a glad whoop.

"Slade! Feller, am I glad to see you. I figured I'd have to unload this shebang. Maybe between the two of us we can get that blasted wheel back on."

"Should be able to," Slade agreed as he dismounted and approached, glancing at the girl, who looked expectantly at Hodson.

"Oh, I forgot," said the puncher. "Marie, this is Walt Slade —I was talking to you about him. Slade, this is Marie, Phil's sister."

There was laughter in Marie Waring's very big and darkly blue eyes as she acknowledged the introduction.

"Really, Mr. Slade," she said, "I seem to have known you for quite a while. You are indeed nearly all that Al and my brother have talked about for the past week."

"Then they gave somebody else a rest," Slade smiled.

The laughter in her eyes spilled over to her red lips, which parted to show little teeth as white and even as Slade's own.

"Oh, what they said was not at all derogatory, just the reverse," she replied.

"How about this blasted wheel?" Hodson broke in. "Maybe with this tree branch for a pry we can manage to lift the wagon and Marie can slide the wheel on the axle."

'I don't think we'll need the pry," Slade differed. "It'll just be in the way. You take the wheel and be ready to slip it on the axle."

"Feller, you can never lift that wagon by yourself," Hodson protested. "I don't believe there is a man in Texas who could do it."

"Remains to be seen," Slade said cheerfully as he bent his knees and gripped the axle with both hands. "Be set with the wheel to shove it on when she comes up."

Slowly he began to straighten. Great muscles leaped out on his arms and shoulders, threatening to burst the fabric of his shirt. And as he straightened, the axle rose until it was parallel to the ground.

"On with the wheel," he said. "Careful, don't pinch my hands. That's right." He shifted his grip. Hodson shoved hard on the wheel, and it slid smoothly into place. Slade eased off till the tire was resting firmly on the ground and stepped back.

Hodson was staring at him unbelievingly. The girl was also staring. The cowboy shook his head.

"Now I've seen everything," he declared.

"Good deal of a trick to it," Slade deprecated the feat.

"Uh-huh, quite a trick," Hodson agreed dryly.

"Got the cap?" Slade asked.

"Yes," said Marie. "I picked it up back along the trail." She handed it to him.

"A wrench?" Slade said to Hodson. "And something that'll do for a pin?"

"I got a box of tools" said the puncher and began rooting about in the wagon to produce them. A few minutes later the cap was firmly in place.

"All set to go," Slade said, wiping the axle grease from his hands with tufts of grass.

Hodson was staring at Shadow, his eyes alight with the real horse lover's admiration.

"Blazes! What a cayuse!" he said. "Never saw his equal. Bet he rides smooth as a baby carriage."

"He does," Slade agreed. He reacted to a sudden impulse aroused by Hodson's enthusiasm.

"Like to fork him for a while?" he added. "I'll handle the team."

"I sure would!" Hdoson exclaimed and turned toward the horse. The great black's ears slanted backward and his eyes rolled.

"It's okay, Shadow," Slade said. The ears pricked forward.

"All right," he said to Hodson. "You won't have any trouble with him."

"Darned if I don't believe he understood just what you said!" exclaimed Hodson.

"He did," Slade answered. "He allows nobody to put a hand on him unless I give the word."

Hodson swung into the saddle and cantered forward joyously. Slade turned to the high seat of the wagon. Marie paused.

"Won't you give me a hand?" she said demurely. "That step is rather high."

Slade laughed, cupped his hands about her slender waist. The next instant she was on the seat, breathless and rosy.

"Good heavens!" she exclaimed. "Do you always handle women like—like a sack of oats?"

"There's a difference," he replied as he mounted beside her and gathered up the reins. "A sack of oats stays put."

"And a woman?"

"She's usually where you don't expect to find her, as of today, for instance," Slade answered.

She laughed. "Yes, riding a peaceful trail, you hardly expected to rescue a damsel in distress, like a knight of old."

"I imagine the knights of old found more women than Holy Grails," he replied, smiling. "Much the same, however, for both are holy."

She regarded him curiously. "Do you really mean that?"

"Of course," he replied. "Without women the world would not go on; they are the source of life."

"I never thought of it in that light, but it is a nice thought," she said. She giggled.

"But they have to have help," she added.

"And *that* is also a nice thought," he said, his eyes dancing.

Miss Waring's long and dark lashes drooped, and she did not answer.

They rolled on, Hodson pacing along ahead, leaning over now and then to talk to Shadow and stroke his glossy neck. The trail had veered slightly to the north, and the low ridge was now not more than four hundred yards distant. Slade, as usual, was constantly scanning his surroundings.

He saw the puff of whitish smoke near the crest of the rise. And even as the spiteful whiplash crack of the distant rifle reached his ears, Al Hodson reeled in the saddle and fell, his face visored with scarlet. Shadow instantly halted and glanced back inquiringly at his master.

Marie screamed. Slade leaped from the wagon, raced to where Shadow stood and slid his Winchester from the saddle boot. He flung the long gun to his shoulder and sprayed the rise crest with bullets, weaving the muzzle back and forth until the rifle was empty. As he shoved fresh cartridges into the magazine he thought he saw a shadow of movement on the crest and sent three quick shots at it. Nothing happened, however, so far as he could see. He turned to where Hodson lay, Marie kneeling beside him. There was a sick feeling in the pit of his stomach as he approached the motionless form; he feared that in obeying a kindly impulse he had sent the cowboy to his death. For there was no doubt in his mind as to whom that slug had been intended for.

13

HOWEVER, he heaved a heartfelt sigh of relief as he drew near. Hodson was muttering and rolling his head from side to side with returning consciousness. As Slade probed the vicinity of the ragged tear just above his right temple, from which blood was still oozing, he opened his eyes and swore feebly.

"Take it easy," Slade told him. "Don't try to sit up yet." He fumbled in his saddle pouch for medicants. A few minutes later the wound was smeared with antiseptic salve, padded and bandaged. Slade wiped the blood from the cowboy's face with a clean hankerchief. He had found no indications of fracture and believed the puncher was not seriously injured.

"Stay with him," he told Marie, and climbed into the wagon. He quickly rearranged the cargo so Hodson could lie down and returned to the patient.

"Think you can sit up now?" he asked.

"Sure," Hodson replied, suiting the action to the word. He held his head in his hands and swore again. Then he grinned wanly. "I'm okay," he said.

Helping him to his feet, Slade led him to the wagon and assisted him to climb aboard.

"All right, stretch out and stay there," he directed. "We'll get you to the ranchhouse and send somebody for the doctor."

"I don't need a doctor," Hodson protested. "I'm okay; you fixed me up fine. It's just a scratch."

"So it appears, but we're taking no chances," Slade replied. "You know there is such a thing as concussion. People receiving head injuries and thinking themselves all right have been known to tumble over a few days later with a stroke. We don't want that to happen. I'll roll you a cigarette, that should help."

"Did you get the blankety-blank?" Hodson asked as he gratefully accepted the brain tablet and puffed vigorously. "I thought I heard you shooting. I don't think I ever really passed out completely."

"I doubt it," Slade answered. "I was shooting blind. I've a

notion he kept on going. If he did, he's gone. If he didn't, let him stay there to poison the coyotes and the buzzards. I'm not going up there to find out. May look the ridge over when I ride back this way, if I am of a mind to."

"But who the devil could it have been?" Hodson wondered. "Eldon Parr ain't no good, but I can't see him going in for this sort of a dry-gulching just because I twitted him about smelling of sheep. And I don't know of anybody else who'd want to down me."

"One tall man atop a black horse looks very much like another," Slade replied pointedly.

Hodson stared at him; so did Marie.

"You—you mean the hellion was after you?" the puncher asked.

Slade shrugged his broad shoulders. "I ride a black horse," he said. "At that distance he couldn't have recognized features."

"I see," Hodson said slowly. "Reckon that outlaw bunch they call the men of steel don't feel over kind toward you after the shellackin' you've given them of late."

"Plausible to think so," Slade conceded.

Hodson swore with fervor. "Excuse me, Marie," he said, "but that's just the way I feel about it."

"Go ahead and don't mind me," the girl told him. "If I had the habit, I'd do some myself."

"Right!" growled Hodson, gingerly feeling his wounded head. "Well, feller, if you need any backin' in your row with those blankety-blanks, count on me. And that'll go for the rest of the boys, and Phil, too."

"And for Marie," Miss Waring added, looking as if she meant it.

"Well, with that kind of backing I don't see how I can lose," Slade smiled. "Now we'll head for home." He climbed onto the seat. Marie took her place beside him.

"Giddap, cayuses," he told the horses. "Some hot coffee will do that punctured gent a lot of good."

The wagon rolled on, Shadow pacing sedately behind. Slade constantly scanned the rises, although he did not think the dry-gulcher had lingered.

In due time they reached the W Diamond ranchhouse, big and old but in an excellent state of repair. Phil Waring was on the veranda, and several of the hands were loitering about the yard. They all came hurrying forward, volleying questions, as Hodson's bandaged head appeared.

Explanations followed, Hodson and Marie doing most of the talking. Waring swore better than Hodson did, and shook hands with Slade.

"Sure hope you got the blankety-blank," he said.

Slade noticed that the owner's left hand and wrist were bandaged.

"What happened to you?" he asked.

"Oh, I was out on the range the other night during that blasted rain," Waring explained. "I was wet and cold and tried to get a fire going under a cliff. Everything was so infernally wet I couldn't make it. So I tore a piece off the tail of my shirt, opened a couple of cartridges and dampened the powder and rubbed it into the rag to make a slow fuse like we use sometimes when blowing water holes. Figured to start the shavings with that. Guess I didn't dampen the powder enough, for it flared and scorched my hand."

"You can lose an eye that way," Slade warned, his own eyes thoughtful.

Waring called a wrangler to care for the horses. He was properly introduced to Shadow, and the big black followed him to the barn. Hodson was led into the living room and made to lie down on a couch, and a hand was ordered to ride to town and fetch the doctor.

"I'll get the coffee going. Soon be time to eat, too," Waring said and headed for the kitchen, Marie accompanying him.

"Phil, just who and what is he?" she asked in low tones.

"Sis, I don't know," her brother replied. "The Mexicans call him El Halcón—The Hawk— and there are folks who say he's an owlhoot."

"I don't believe it," she declared flatly.

"To tell the truth, I don't either," Waring conceded. "Sheriff Ross and Doc Price seem to think mighty well of him, and Mig Lopez and Froglip Fogarty cottoned to him right away. The Mexicans swear he's God's right-hand man, and judging from the things he's done since he coiled his twine here, I've a notion they may be closest to the right of it."

"Yes, I think they are," Marie said. "Anyhow, I think he is the handsomest man I ever laid eyes on, and the most charming."

Her brother chuckled. "Careful," he said warningly. "He's all of that, but he's also the sort that always has his eyes on the next hilltop; remember that."

"I'll try hard to forget it," she retorted. "And you're trying to get him to sign on as range boss, aren't you?"

"If I can argue him into taking it," Waring answered.

"I'll add my powers of persuasion to yours," she promised. "Felipe, start the coffee heating," she told the cook, a Mexican, and was inspired to add, "We have El Halcón as a guest."

The old cook's eyes widened, and he bowed his head. "It is as if our Lord paused to break bread with us," he said simply.

"See?" said Waring.

"Yes, I see," she replied slowly.

They returned to the living room. Marie went upstairs. Slade and Waring smoked and talked, while Hodson drowsed on the couch. He roused up to say, "Slade, tell him about that wrecked ship you and Lopez found; folks were talking about it in town."

"How's that?" Waring asked. Slade gave an account of the incident, to which Waring listened intently.

"Wonder what they were after?" he remarked when Slade paused. "Never can tell about those Gulf ships; they pack all sorts of stuff. Some of it the Customs people never get a look at. Must have been something worthwhile. Reckon the poor devils on the ship never had a chance."

"It looked that way," Slade agreed.

"And they set a false beacon to lure her onto the rocks," Waring said thoughtfully. "But how in blazes did they get on and off without leaving any tracks?"

"I'd like to have the answer to that one, but I haven't got it," Slade replied.

Marie came down at that moment. She wore a dress that Slade thought set off the sweet lines of her small figure admirably. Her glossy curls were neatly brushed, her eyes were bright, and there was a touch of color in each creamily tanned cheek.

"Gosh!" Waring exclaimed with brotherly tact, "first time I've seen you in anything but overalls and a shirt for a month."

She met Slade's laughing gaze, and the color in her cheeks deepened.

"The boys are coming in—time to eat," said Waring. "Come on, Slade, you'll have to take potluck."

The "potluck" was highly satisfactory, for old Felipe outdid himself in deference to the honored guest.

Dinner was a hilarious affair. The hands twitted Hodson about his injury and flatly refused to believe his version of the affair as vouched for by Slade and Marie.

"You're just covering up for the horned toad," they declared. "We know what happened. Drunk, fell out of the wagon and cracked his skull. Lucky he landed on his head, otherwise he might have got hurt. Skull's just like a terrapin's —solid bone all the way through."

They waited anxiously for the verdict, however, when Doc Price arrived a couple of hours after dark. The old practitioner glowered at Slade.

"Might have known it," he said. "No rest when you're around."

"But, Doc, you don't want to be arrested for vagrancy, do you? No visible means of support," the Ranger protested.

"Don't worry about me," said Doc. "I put one over on the undertaker. Signed a partnership agreement with him the minute you showed up. We'll both get rich. All right, Hodson, let's have a look.

"A good chore of padding and bandaging," he nodded to Slade. "Nothing to worry about, just a scalp cut. He'll be looking for a chance to get hanged tomorrow. Hope he makes it. Sure I'll spend the night, Waring. Should be some business for me before morning, with Slade here. I brought all of my tools when I heard he was squattin' with you."

"It would seem you are a rather terrible person, though you seem so nice, Mr. Slade," Marie said.

"Really, I don't deserve such a reputation," El Halcón protested. "Doctors are always prone to exaggerate. That's to keep the patient's mind off his troubles."

"Patients don't have troubles—they unload 'em on the doctor," Price grunted. "Where do I sleep tonight, Phil?"

"Same room you always use, next to mine down the hall," Waring replied. "Sis, give Slade the big room at the head of the stairs. Show him to it so he can stow his pouches.

"That's the one you'll sleep in if you sign up as range boss," he added to Slade. "I'd rather have you here than in the bunkhouse, so you'll be handy in case I need you."

"And we figure to have a little poker game in the bunkhouse tonight," Al Hodson said. "Care to join us, Slade?"

"Be glad to," the Ranger accepted. "Haven't looked at a pasteboard for quite a while." Marie made a moue at him.

"Come along first, Mr. Slade, and I'll show you your room," she said. They mounted the stairs, and she opened a door to show a wide and airy room, comfortably furnished.

"Hope you'll like it," she said.

"I know I will," he replied.

"And do you intend to sign up with us, Mr. Slade?" she asked.

"The offer becomes more and more attractive all the time," he conceded smilingly. "Incidentally, an owner usually addresses a range boss by his first name and does away with the Mister."

"I hope you'll find it still more attractive—Walt," she said softly. "And, seeing as I am only a half-owner, I think we can dispense with the Miss."

"All right—Marie," he replied. "Yes, it *is* steadily becoming more attractive."

"Have luck at your poker game," she said. She led the way downstairs, where the hands were awaiting him.

"How about you settin' in, Doc?" Hodson asked.

"Not me," that worthy declined unequivocally. "All right for you young whippersnappers to sit up all night, but I expect work to do tomorrow."

Waring also declined, citing a similar reason. Slade and the others trooped out.

The poker game lasted until after midnight. Slade enjoyed it, for he liked poker. He managed to stay about even, which was what he wished to do.

When he reached the ranchhouse, he found a low light burning in the living room. Curled up in an easy chair was Marie Waring, the light striking glints of gold in her tawny hair.

"I waited up for you," she said, unnecessarily.

"Nice of you," Slade smiled. "I'm glad you did."

"I wished to talk to you about several things," she said. "First, something I think you should know before you sign up with us, if you decide to do so."

"Yes?" Slade asked expectantly.

"Yes. Very likely you will hear things said about my brother. Things which I assure you are not true. Phil was rather wild when he was younger, before our father died, and was in trouble a few times. But he is honest, and he doesn't lie."

"How could he be otherwise with such a charming advocate," Slade parried. He was thinking of Miguel Lopez' rather vague remark anent Phil Waring, which ended with—"but I don't spread gossip." He decided that a direct question was in order.

"Just what is being said of him?" he asked.

"Somehow, by somebody, it seems a whisper started," she replied slowly, "that Phil is connected with the so-called men of steel you exposed. That he is their leader. I hope you won't believe it."

"I never take much stock in what's said about a person, especially if it isn't said to his face; I make a habit of finding out for myself before passing judgment," the Ranger replied, again not definitely committing himself.

For again he was thinking—thinking of Phil Waring's burned hand and the false beacon lighted to lure a ship to destruction, the wood of which must have been drenched with oil to cause it to flare up brightly despite the rain.

"And what I've told you wouldn't deter you from signing on with us?" she asked.

"Not in the least, if I decide to do so," he said, and meant it.

She sighed. "I feel better," she said. "You are a comforting person to have around. I think you always learn the truth. But it's late, and you must be tired." She extinguished the light, and they groped their way to the stairs.

"Be careful and don't stumble," she whispered, with a little giggle. "We'll wake the whole house."

For answer, he picked her up, cradled her in his arms and carried her up the steps. At the head of the stairs their lips met.

14

The cowboys trooping in for breakfast awakened Slade. For some minutes he lay reviewing the happenings of the past twenty-four hours. Then he got up, washed and dressed, for he wished to get an early start back to town.

Deciding he could go another day without a shave, he descended the stairs to find Marie and her brother in the living room.

"We waited to eat with you," said Waring. "Come on, before I tumble over from starvation. Doc ate and headed for town. Said he had patients to look after."

Waring and Slade chatted while they ate, but Marie sat silent, her eyes downcast, the color coming and going in her soft cheeks.

"Why you so quiet?" Waring asked. "Usually it's impossible to get a word in edgewise when you're around."

"I was just—thinking," she replied. She looked up, met Slade's eyes, blushed rosy-red and dropped her gaze to her plate.

"Sorry you have to rush off, Slade," Waring remarked. "I'd hoped you'd ride over the holding with me today."

"I want another look at that wrecked ship before she breaks up completely," Slade explained. "If a storm comes along, she's liable to do just that."

Marie looked up quickly. "I'd like to see it," she said. "May I ride with you?"

Slade hesitated. "All right, if your brother doesn't object."

"Lots of good it would do me to object," grunted Waring. "She does as she pleases. But you'll be mighty late getting back," he added.

"I'll stay overnight in town, at the hotel," she replied.

"Okay," said her brother. "Go to it. You'll be in good hands, anyhow. Slade won't let anything happen to you."

Marie shot him a sideways glance through her lashes and smiled slightly.

Half an hour later they rode off together, Marie dressed in neat Levi's and a soft blue shirt, open low at the throat.

"I hope you don't mind, but I hate to ride in fussy things," she said.

"That's sensible," he replied. "Besides, you look very nice as you are; and as I told you before, you look very, very nice in—anything."

Marie smiled and dimpled. "I'm glad you feel that way about—that," she said softly.

As they rode, Slade constantly scanned their surroundings with care, although he did not really expect a reoccurence of the day before's happening. They had covered something less than half the distance to town when he suddenly pulled up, gazing northward.

Over the ridge, some four hundred yards distant, dark shapes were wheeling and soaring and steadily drifting lower to settle out of sight behind the tall brush.

"You stay here," he told his companion. "I want to look at that rise."

She stared at him, wide-eyed. "Those—those are vlutures, are they not?" she asked.

"They are," he replied grimly and spoke to Shadow.

It did not take the powerful horse long to force his way through the brush to the ridge crest. Slade abruptly pulled him to a halt. The disturbed vultures croaked angrily and took to the air. Slade didn't feel too good; the remains of a vultures' feast is not nice to look upon.

The coyotes had been there, too, and there was little left of the dry-gulcher but bones and clothing shredded by beak and fang.

"So I did get the hellion," he muttered. "Shadow, there should be a horse around here somewhere."

At that moment, a plaintive whinny sounded, and he saw the horse, peering around a bush. A saddle hung askew, and a broken bit strap dangled.

Slade dismounted and approached the animal, which showed no signs of fright. He removed the saddle and the bit so the creature would be comfortable until somebody picked it up.

Then he stepped back and gazed at the brand scoring its hide. It was an HF Bar.

"That makes three of those east Texas burns," he told Shadow. "Remember, two of the horses ridden by the members of the bunch we downed by the bay were HF Bar. This is getting a mite interesting. Stretching coincidence a bit to think they were all bought or stolen over there. Looks like several of the gents known as the men of steel were from east Texas, Neches River country." He turned the black's head and rode back to where Marie waited. She looked at him questioningly.

"Yes, he's up there, what's left of him," he said.

"I'm glad," she said, clenching her little fist. "He meant to murder you. He got just what was coming to him."

"I'll have to admit I don't feel particularly conscious-stricken about it," he replied. "He did nearly get Hodson. If Al hadn't leaned forward to stroke Shadow's neck when he did, the slug would have drilled him dead center instead of just creasing him. Yes, the world can do without that sort."

Marie reached down and tapped the walnut stock protruding from her saddle boot.

"You see, I brought my rifle along," she said. "I can shoot, and I hope I get a chance to use it."

"Never mind," Slade said. "I don't want to take any chances on a corpse and cartridge session with you along. You're too precious."

Miss Waring tossed her reddish curls. "Oh, I'm just another woman," she replied. "And what is one woman among so many."

"Now who's been telling you things about me?" he teased.

"I don't need to be *told*," she answered airily. "A demonstration in practice is more convincing than precept."

Slade appeared to understand perfectly the rather vague observation, for he chuckled, and the devils of laughter in the back of his cold eyes turned gleeful somersaults. Marie smiled and blushed.

They rode on, Slade vigilant and alert, Marie apparently occupied with retrospect, which appeared to be pleasant, judging from the coming and going dimple at the corner of her red mouth.

Arriving in town without incident, Slade replenished the store of provisions in his saddle pouches.

"You'll be hungry before we get back, so we'll cook out and have a snack," he told the girl.

"That will be fun," she said. "I love a dying campfire at night."

After pausing at the Post Hole for a cup of coffee, they headed south through brilliant sunshine, Marie riding a big roan that looked to have speed and endurance. He was a mettlesome horse, but the way she handled him evoked Slade's admiration.

"I could ride before I could walk," she replied to his comment. "I love horses and can always get along with them."

"You have the trick of voice as well as of hand," he said. "And that is most important. Talk to a horse in a way he can understand, and you can get anything from him."

"I guess the same goes for a woman," she smiled. "Anyhow, it worked." They laughed together.

They did not push their horses, and the sun was low in the west when they sighted the ship. She hadn't changed much, so far as Slade could ascertain.

"I think they'll be able to salvage her if they don't waste too much time and get here before there's a bad blow," he observed. "She's wedged tight between those two reefs, which protect her to an extent. And that hole in her bow appears to be all the real damage she has suffered."

"It looks so lonely and forlorn," Marie remarked.

"A beached ship always does," Slade replied. "She's out of her element."

With interest, he noted that the stretch of placid water beyond the bow was now in motion, moving slowly to sea. However, the tide was runing out, and he did not attach any significance to the phenomenon. That is, till a moment later, when a puzzling incident developed.

Bobbing along on the surface was a small white cylinder; it was a half-smoked cigarette.

"Now where did that come from?" he wondered, glancing perplexedly about. "There's nobody on the shore, and it couldn't have come from any great distance—wouldn't take long for the paper to get soaked and it would sink. See, it's beginning to disintegrate now."

It was. Another moment and the paper had shredded away, releasing brown particles of tobacco. Almost immediately, both paper and tobacco vanished. Slade continued to gaze about, following the strip of moving water with his eyes. It ended in a jumble of overhanging rocks which faced the shoreline.

"Guess the wind must have blown it from somewhere," he hazarded, knowing that the explanation really didn't explain, for the wind was blowing in from the bay. With a shake of his head, he returned his attention to the vessel.

"I've a notion Sheriff Ross has learned her registry by now, and perhaps who are her owners," he said. "May have gotten in touch with them. Yes, I believe she can be salvaged. Hope so; I hate to see a ship die. Bad enough that the crew had to."

"You are convinced they were murdered, are you not?" Marie asked.

"I am," he replied. "I suppose the bodies were carried out to sea. I've been watching the shoreline all the way down here, and there was certainly no sign of them. The tide will sometimes bring a body back to shore, and there are strong currents running in all the time."

Marie shuddered. "Something uncanny about a body coming back that way," she said. "Looks almost as if it were seeking rest."

Slade nodded and resumed his study of the beetling, clifflike rocks which fronted the shoreline a little distance to the east. Because of the angle of the curvature and the overhang configuration of the rocks, he could only see about halfway down to the waterline. Abruptly he turned to face his companion.

"I'm going to climb down those rocks," he told her. "I want to get a look at their base."

"All right, I'll go with you," she replied.

"You'll stay right where you are," he said.

"I won't," she declared flatly. "Don't worry about me; I can climb as well as you can. I've done lots of it."

"Okay," he surrendered. "But if I get all wet fishing you out of the water, I'll spank you."

"Don't tempt me!" she giggled. "Come on, let's go."

It really wasn't an extremely difficult chore, for the rough contours provided plenty of handholds and footrests. Getting over the bulge of the overhang was a bit tricky, but they negotiated it without mishap.

Very quickly Slade dismissed his fears for his companion; she was active as a cat and, as she said, had undoubtedly done rough climbing before.

After a while, going carefully and slowly, they were well down the rugged face. Slade suddenly uttered an exclamation. Now he could see to the water's edge, and almost below them was an opening in the rocks, something resembling a partially submerged railroad tunnel. The opening was perhaps thirty feet in width and the lip of the rock roof a good ten feet above the surface of the water.

"Look," Marie said, "there's another one a little farther along."

She was right. Another and similiar opening showed some twenty or thirty yards farther east. Slade studied both openings with interest.

Water was rushing into the farther opening, quite briskly, while from the near one water flowed out placidly, which facts he pointed out to his companion.

"What do you make of it, Walt?" she asked.

"I'd say," he replied judiciously, "that those openings are the mouths of caves hollowed out in this limestone formation by the action of water in the course of many ages."

"But why does water run into one and out of the other?" she persisted.

"I'd say that the far cave or tunnel has an inward slope, while this one has an outward slope."

"And—" she prompted.

"It would appear," he explained, "that somewhere, quite a distance back under the ground, the two caves merge. The water flowing in is perhaps shunted aside by an end wall or some similar formation into the cave with the outward slope. That's the plausible hydraulic explanation."

"Sort of a watery merry-go-round," Marie commented.

He chuckled at the aptness of her expression. "Sort of," he agreed. "But I still want to know where that blasted cigarette butt came from."

"You said you thought maybe the wind blew it into the water," she reminded him.

"That could be the answer, possibly," he conceded, but without conviction. In truth, he knew it was proof positive that somewhere, somehow, somebody had access to those underground currents. "Let's be getting back topside."

They made the return climb without accident. On level ground, Slade turned and gazed toward the rises to the north, fully a half mile distant. After a long look he turned back to his companion.

"We'll ride on down around the bend to that broad sand dune where we had the ruckus with the sheep thieves," he decided. "Back in the thickets is a good place to cook and eat. A spring there, and grass."

"Good!" she exclaimed. "I'm starved."

They reached the mesa in due time. Slade soon got a fire going. He heaped on plenty of fuel so it would burn down to a bed of coals favorable for cooking. He took his rolled blanket from behind his saddle and spread it on the ground nearby.

"For you to sit on," he explained.

Next he loosened the cinches and flipped out the bits so the horses could graze and drink in comfort. By the time he had emptied the saddle pouches of their contents, the fire was in good shape.

"All right," Marie said, "I'll do the cooking; that's woman's work. Oh, I know how; I've prepared many a meal over a campfire. You just take it easy for a while."

Nothing loath to do so, he stretched out comfortably on the blanket and rolled a cigarette, smoking leisurely till she called him to come and eat.

Bread, coffee, bacon and eggs. Simple, but plenty of everything. And for the appetite of youth and perfect health, a feast.

They ate slowly, talking and laughing, and it was full dark before the utensils were cleaned and packed back in the pouches. Then they sat by the dying fire, mostly silent, for the drowsy peace and the wild beauty of the wastelands seemed to make talk superfluous.

The flame sank lower and lower to glowing embers, which in turn dulled and tarnished till only a little cluster of sparks remained. These winked out slowly, one by one.

"Look!" Marie whispered laughingly. "The children are getting out of school. There they go, one by one." A moment later, "And there goes the teacher, the very last one. School's over for the day!"

The darkness closed down like a soft and gentle blanket. Overhead, the glittering stars smiled a benediction. There was not a breath of wind, and the little waves at the base of the mesa pulsed rhythmically back and forth with hushed murmurings and whisperings. The descending wings of sleep hovered over the tired earth.

15

SUDDENLY SLADE SAT FORWARD in an attitude of listening. To his keen ears had come a sound, faint but unmistakeable—the beat of horses' hoofs drawing steadily nearer from the east.

"I want to see who that is," he said to the girl. Rising, he glided silently through the growth to where he could get a view of the trail. And just as silently, Marie glided behind him.

Back of the final straggle they halted. The sound of hoofs grew louder, and they could hear an occasional mutter of voices. Huge, grotesque in the wan starlight, some eight or ten horsemen loomed. They rode at a slow pace, lounging comfortably in their saddles, advancing slowly but purposefully, as if they had a definite goal in view but were in no hurry to get there. They drifted past the two watchers and continued on into the west. Slade breathed deeply, half turned, hesitated. Marie instantly divined what was in his mind.

"You want to follow those men, don't you, Walt?" she whispered.

"I'd like to," he admitted. "I'd sure like to know who they are and where they're headed, but I can't take the chance. Can't leave you here alone."

"You're going to take me with you," she declared resolutely.

"I couldn't take the chance," he repeated. "Something might happen. I—"

"Listen," she broke in, "you believe those men are up to no good, don't you?"

"I can't help but feel that way," he conceded.

"You think they are the outlaw bunch that has been terrorizing the section?"

"Yes," he admitted reluctantly.

"All right," she said. "Then I have a personal interest in the matter. I am a property owner, and my property is not safe with that sort mavericking around. We're going to find out what they're up to, and if it isn't good, we're going to stop it. Come on, or I'll ride alone."

"You're a blasted problem," he sighed. "But you are a girl to ride the river with." She laughed softly, for she had just received the highest compliment the rangeland can pay.

"One thing, though, or we don't move," he added. "When I ask you to do something, do it and don't argue."

Once again the smile and the dimple. "Well, do you think it's necessary to bring that up? Compliance has gotten to be a habit. Let's go!"

Swiftly they tightened the cinches and slipped the bits back into the mouths of the full-fed and rested horses and rode out of the thicket.

"Do you think you can trail them in the dark?" Marie asked doubtfully. "They must be quite a ways ahead of us by now."

"I think I can," he answered. "Just west of here is a wide bend, and the trail is brush-flanked on both sides. We can speed up until we round the bend. They're taking it easy, and by then I figure we should sight them in the starlight. They're riding in the open, and I doubt if they are paying much attention to their back trail. We'll keep in the shadow and as far back as possible. Here we go."

They sent the horses forward at a fast clip and did not slow down until they were close to the far end of the curve. As Slade expected, when they reached a straight stretch which ran for nearly a mile, they could just make out the dim shapes of the quarry, still proceeding at a leisurely pace.

They followed, hugging the edge of the trail, taking advantage of every bit of cover that offered. All along there were straggles of chaparral, so it was not hard to escape observation, especially as the riders ahead never appeared to look back.

The miles flowed under the horses' irons, the great clock in the sky wheeled westward. The quarry continued to advance steadily. Then, abruptly, the horsemen turned sharply to the right.

"I know where that trail leads to," Slade told his companion. "Sebastian Hernandez pointed it out to me the other day. It leads to the Telo holding north of Miguel Lopez'. This is getting interesting."

Approaching the forks cautiously, they again sighted the quarry, a little farther ahead, apparently having speeded up. Another two miles and Slade knew they were on the Telo range.

Again the horsemen swerved, this time onto the open pasture. They slowed their pace. And now Slade had a problem on his hands. To follow across the prairie would be reckless to the point of foolhardiness. If one of the riders chanced to look back, he couldn't help spotting them.

Then he saw that a little to the north was a long straggle of growth paralleling and only a few hundred yards distant from where the quarry rode.

"We'll slide in behind that brush," he told Marie. "Maybe our ears will tell us the course they're following, or perhaps we can slip along in the edge of the chaparral and keep them in sight."

When they reached the bristle of growth, he found that they could do just that, at the cost of a few thorn scratches. By careful maneuvering, they were able to keep the group in sight and at the same time remain concealed themselves.

"This is easy," he whispered to Marie. "That is, if your cayuse doesn't take a notion to sing a song to the stars. I don't have to worry about Shadow."

"Rojo is usually a very quiet horse," she breathed back.

And then abruptly things were not so easy. The horsemen ahead were veering toward the brush; soon they were at its edge and practically invisible to the two trailers.

"Now what the devil are they up to?" Slade muttered. "Surely they didn't spot us."

"Listen," Marie whispered. "Isn't that a sheep bleating?"

"It is," Slade said. "I'm beginning to catch on; they aim to grab off a flock of Telo's woollies. We can risk riding ahead; they won't pull up till they're opposite the flock, I hope. Blast it! I'm worried about you."

"Save your worry," she replied. "I'll be all right. Look, I believe I see the flock, only a few hundred yards from where they must be riding."

"Yes, that's the flock, all right," Slade agreed. "The hellions will be riding out in another minute or two to round them up and start them moving. Then we'll see."

"I hope—" Marie began. "Oh, good heavens!"

Directly ahead, all hell had broken loose. From the edge of the growth came a bellow of gunfire. And from the tall grass near the huddled sheep came answering orange flashes.

"Unfork!" Slade snapped. "Lie flat on the ground. The fool herders who were guarding the flock stayed out in the open instead of holing up in the brush. They won't have a chance. Down flat and cut loose with your rifle. Fire as fast as you can. Doesn't matter if you don't score a hit. Just make all the racket you can."

He flung his own Winchester to his shoulder as he spoke and sprayed the edge of the growth ahead with lead. At the same time his great voice pealed forth in a stentorian roar.

"Let 'em have it, boys, let 'em have it! Don't let one of the hellions get away! Let 'em have it!"

Marie chimed in, raising her normally soft contralto to a powerful screech. Added to the booming of the two rifles, the uproar was deafening. From the herders in the grass came triumphant whoops, intermingled with yells of pain. And the growth ahead erupted in a veritable pandemonium. Yells, screams, curses made the night hideous. Then there was a prodigious crashing in the brush and a thunder of hoofs as the raiders fled wildly.

"Call to the herders and tell them who we are," Slade said. Whirling, he raced through the narrow belt of growth, heedless of thorns and trailing branches. But when he reached the far edge, the demoralized rustlers were but blurs on the prairie to the north. He emptied his rifle in their general direction to speed them on their way and returned through the chaparral to find Marie surrounded by half a dozen wildly excited herders, one limping, another cursing under his breath as he cherished a blood-drenched upper arm.

"Got a lantern?" Slade asked, stilling their chatter.

"*Sí, Capitán,* we have one."

"Fetch it and light it, and a couple of you scout the brush over there and see if we knocked off any of the hellions. Doubt if we did—it was blind shooting—but take a look, anyhow. Careful—one of that sort wounded is as dangerous as a broken-backed rattler."

"He won't be dangerous for long," came the grim answer.

Slade whistled to Shadow, who trotted out of the brush, snorting his disgust with the whole proceeding. With bandage and salve from the pouches, Slade went to work on the wounded, whose hurts, he decided, were painful but not serious.

The two searchers returned from the growth to report no success in their hunt for possible bodies.

"The next time you're set to guard a flock, hole up in the brush instead of lying in the grass out in the opening where you're setting quail," Slade told the group. "If we hadn't happened along when we did, you'd have been gone goslings."

"*Sí,* it is so," was answered. "We are indeed of the many who owe life to El Halcón."

"And don't forget the little *señorita,*" Slade reminded them. "She did her share."

Sombreros swept the ground in salute.

"And now, *Capitán*, you must ride with the wounded to the *hacienda* to spend the night," said the leader of the herders. "The *partrón* will want to thank you for what you did in his behalf. It is late, and the *hacienda* is less than five miles distant."

"Reckon we'll have to," Slade conceded. "Let me have the lantern," he told the herder. "I want to look over the ground where the devils were holed up."

It was not difficult to locate the spot. The panicked raiders had torn down plenty of brush making their getaway. Slade went over the ground with meticulous care.

"We nicked some of them," he told the herders when he returned. "I found quite a few blood spots. Some of them were bright and frothy, denoting arterial blood. Looks like somebody got rather hard hit. Anyhow, we threw them completely off balance and they hightailed like the Devil beating tanbark."

"Think you, *Capitán*, that they might come back?" the herder asked apprehensively.

"Under the circumstances, would you?" Slade countered. The herder grinned and shook his head.

"Now to the *hacienda* we must go," he said.

The ride to the ranchhouse was comparatively short, and although the pace was slow in deference to the wounded herders, they were not long in reaching it. Hammering on the door, they quickly aroused the household. Alfredo Telo, big, portly and jolly, appeared in a long nightshirt and an old-fashioned nightcap. His gratitude was profuse, and he thanked Slade and Marie over and over.

"The loss of the flock I could have put up with," he said. "But not the loss of my men. Most of them have been with me for years and are looked upon as part of my family. I am deeply in your debt, Mr. Slade. Ha! Here is my wife; she will care for *la señorita*. But first food and hot coffee. Doubtless you are hungry—the young are always hungry. I am not young, but I have that trait in common with youth."

Mrs. Telo, plump and motherly, immediately repaired to the kitchen, where the cook, awakened with the rest, was already busy rattling pots and pans. The wounded herders were made as comfortable as possible, and a *vaquero* was dispatched to town to fetch the doctor.

The Telos, like Lopez and Garcia, were of the best Texas-Mexican stock, and Slade liked them at once. Soon they sat down to a bountiful meal to which all did full justice.

"And now to bed with both of you," Mrs. Telo told Slade and Marie. "Young people need their rest."

"Then you also had better get back to bed," Slade replied gallantly. Mrs. Telo smiled a very youthful smile.

"Our son is older than you," she said. "Old people don't need so much rest; they stay up, watching the stars, to which they are soon going."

16

SLADE FOUND HE WAS wearier than he thought, and it was mid-morning when he awakened to a feeling of well being. Not only had he frustrated the attempted wide-looping of the sheep and the murder of the herders, but he was beginning to get a nebulous idea as to the solution of the mystery of the vanished stock. The thing seemed incredible, but he believed the theory he had developed after viewing the rock formation near the wrecked vessel might well be sound. Anyhow, he resolved to put it to a test as soon as possible.

Descending to the living room, he found Marie already up. "Oh, I had it easier than you did," she replied when he commented on her early rising. "You had the responsibility of— looking after me."

"Well, did I discharge that responsibility in a satisfactory manner?" he asked, his eyes smiling.

"You did," she answered, with emphasis. "Come on, breakfast is waiting and I'm starved, as usual."

After breakfast, Slade examined the wounded herders and was satisfied with their condition.

"When Doc gets here he'll put on a few finishing touches and you'll be okay," he told them. "And now, Marie, it's time we were heading for home. Your brother will be pawing sod for fair."

"Chances are he won't even miss me, and if he does, he'll just conclude that I decided to spend the day in town," she replied. "Don't worry about Phil—he's used to me."

Slade chuckled. "I'm beginning to understand what he's had to put up with all these years," he said.

"Not so many," she retorted. "Remember, I've just turned twenty-one."

When they were out of sight of the ranchhouse, after the Telos had called down blessings on them and commended them to the care of St. Julian, the patron saint of travelers, Slade said, "Mind if we take a roundabout way home? Will make us a bit late."

"The longer, the better," Marie returned cheerfully.

Instead of following the track to the main Lavaca trail, Slade turned north across the prairie. By doing so, he figured he could cut the route followed by the fleeing raiders the night before.

With the instinct of the plainsman for distance and direction, he had no difficulty reaching the spot where they had burst from the belt of growth. And here the trail they left was easy enough to follow—that is, to the eyes of El Halcón.

For a while the track continued due north. Then, after the rustlers had slowed their breakneck pace, it veered east, as he figured it would.

They rode east at a good pace, for Slade was confident he knew exactly the route the bunch would follow, the same route followed by Garcia's stolen flock. He was anxious to be sure, however, and was highly pleased to learn that he was right.

The miles flowed past, and at length they sighted the strip of sandy, semi-arid land. To Slade's satisfaction, the tracks ran straight to it.

"Here we turn south to the Lavaca trail," he told Marie. "No sense in crossing that hot patch."

"Did you learn what you hoped to, Walt?" she asked curiously.

"Yes, that they continued due east," he replied, turning Shadow's nose. He did not tell her what else he believed he had learned. Corroborating his deductions was a chore for him alone.

It was well past dark when they reached Port Lavaca, and the town's lights twinkled a friendly welcome.

"And I'm hungry again," Marie said plaintively.

"We'll eat as soon as we care for the horses," he replied. "Looks like you're stuck a night in town, after all. Well, there should be vacant rooms at the hotel."

"Convenient," she commented, with a sideways glance through her lashes.

Slade gave the tired horses a good rubdown and made sure all their needs were provided for. Afterwards they repaired to the Post Hole, to find it lively and gay, as usual. While they were eating, Sheriff Ross came in and occupied a chair at their table.

"Well, did you learn anything about the ship?" Slade asked. The sheriff nodded.

"Spanish registry, American agents at Galveston. Sailed from Tampico, Mexico, with cargo of hides and tallow. Presumably bound for Galveston. What she was doing in Matagorda Bay nobody seems to know. Agents disavow any knowledge. They are sending a salvage crew to see what can be done about her."

Slade nodded thoughtfully. "She can be salvaged, if they show up ahead of a storm," he said. "Looks like she was conducting a little clandestine trading on the side."

"Uh-huh, smuggling I'd say," replied the sheriff. "Well, that angle is up to the Customs people."

"Yes," Slade conceded. "But the wrecking and, presumably, killings took place on Texas soil, which concerns Texas peace officers." Ross nodded gloomy agreement.

"Did you learn what crew she carried?" Slade asked.

"Captain, mate and crew of eleven," Ross replied.

"Check," Slade said. "There were eleven duffelbags in the forecastle, the crew's quarters."

"Any notion how the hellions got on and off the ship without leaving any tracks?" Ross asked.

"I'm beginning to get one," Slade answered. "Will discuss it later, when I get the loose ends tied up. That is, if they'll tie. I may be way off trail."

"Never knew you to be," grunted the sheriff.

"Always a first time," Slade returned cheerfully. Marie glanced at him sideways and smiled.

"Well, what have you two been up to?" the sheriff asked. "I heard Doc Price rode south this morning, so I figured Slade must have started a ruckus somewhere, seeing as he was down in that direction."

Marie told him, and the story from her lips lost nothing in the telling, especially the part Slade played. The sheriff shook his head in wordless admiration.

"With only a gal to lend a hand, he stampedes a whole herd of owlhoots," he said when Marie paused for breath. "Feller, you're the limit."

"The girl lent a very helping hand," Slade said. "She made more racket than a dozen. I figured those sheep thieves thought a banshee was after them, especially if there happened to be any of Irish descent in their number."

"Is my voice that bad?" Marie asked in shocked tones.

"Normally it's as sweet as a nightingale singing on the Tree of Paradise, but when you take a notion to screech, it sounds like a coyote carnival in an owl's nest," Slade replied.

Sheriff Ross shook with laughter. Marie appeared to turn the matter over in her mind.

"He always leavens any compliment he pays," she said at

length. "One moment he'll say my hair is as a forest pool brim-ful of sunset, the next that it reminds him of a scrambled egg. What is a girl supposed to do with such a man?"

"Well, I could offer a number of suggestions, but I think you're capable of handling the matter yourself," the sheriff answered. "But talking of scrambled eggs makes me hungry. Waiter!"

After the sheriff finished his meal, Marie said, "I'm tired. Mind if I go to bed?"

"A good notion," Slade answered. "I'm going to follow your example before long; it's been a busy week. I'll walk you to the hotel; I have to register for a room, too. See you in the morning before we head for the ranchhouse, Neale."

The hotel desk clerk, who knew Marie well, called her by name.

"I'll give you Number Twelve, the room you usually have, Miss Waring," he said. "Mr. Slade, you can have Thirteen, if you're not superstitious."

"I've always considered thirteen my lucky number," Slade replied. Marie smiled.

After breakfast the following morning, Slade said, "I want to see Ross a few minutes before we ride."

"All right, dear, I'll wait for you in the hotel lobby," Marie answered. "Take your time."

When he reached the office, Slade found the sheriff just leaving.

"I'm going over to the packing house and see if I can locate Parr," he explained. "Yesterday one of Garcia's hands rode in with a message about a flock Garcia is getting ready to trail. Parr was off somewhere, so I offered to relay the message. Like to come along?"

"Yes, I would," Slade replied.

At the packing house they failed to find the owner. "He hasn't been here since yesterday morning," the superintendent, an affable person, said. "Glad to know you, Mr. Slade. Would you like to look over the plant while you wait for Mr. Parr?"

Slade signified that he would, and the super showed them around, explaining the various angles of the business. Finally they came to a small room where men were soldering big sheets of tin into cylinders, one end of which they capped.

"For canned mutton," the superintendent said. "Something of a novelty, but it's going over well. Mr. Parr has progressive ideas."

"He certainly has," Slade conceded, and meant it. There

was a glow in his eyes as they returned to the office to await Eldon Parr.

However, after waiting a while without Parr putting in an appearance, Slade decided to leave.

"I want to get Marie back home," he explained. "I'm afraid her brother will be worried. I'll be seeing you tomorrow, I expect."

Without delay, he got the rigs on the horses and rejoined Marie. They reached the W Diamond ranchhouse before noon to find Phil Waring puttering about the yard.

"Hello, have a nice ride?" he greeted them, and immediately started talking about something else.

"Remember what I told you?" Marie said to Slade, after Phil had headed for the kitchen to tell the cook to rustle his hocks. "He doesn't even realize that we've been gone two nights instead of one. I guess all men are impossible."

"I won't forget either of them," he protested.

"I hope not," she said, with a sigh. "And you'll think of me sometimes, when you're riding over the next hilltop?" she added, her eyes suddenly wistful.

"Yes," he replied.

"Come and get it, or we'll throw it away!" Phil shouted, appearing from the kitchen before Slade could say more.

At the table, Marie recounted their adventures for the benefit of her brother, who listened with absorbed interest.

"Must have been quite a shindig," he chuckled. "Wish I could have been there with you."

"I tried to keep her out of it, but it was no go," Slade remarked.

"Try and keep her out of anything!" Waring snorted. "I gave up years ago. She's stubborn as a blue-nosed mule when she takes a notion to be, and twice as contrary. And you figure it was the same bunch that was gallivanting around in tin shirts?"

"Undoubtedly," Slade said. "They have changed their dress, but not their mode of operation; leave no witnesses alive appears to be their motto. Killers of the worst sort."

"Uh-huh, all of that," Waring nodded. "But I've a notion they're going to get their comeuppance, and soon," he predicted.

Later, when they were alone, Marie gave the Ranger a bit of a start with an unexpected remark.

"Walt," she said, "I purposely refrained from mentioning those cave mouths in the rocks to Phil and Neale Ross. I have a feeling you prefer not to have them talked about."

"I do, for the time being at least," he admitted. "Don't miss much, do you?"

"A woman must develop a certain sympathetic understanding where a man is concerned, if she hopes to hold his regard," she replied.

He nodded sober agreement. "You're right," he conceded. "Unfortunately, many do not."

At that moment, Waring entered. "What say, Walt, like to take a little ride with me and look things over?" he suggested.

"Not a bad notion," the Ranger replied. "Let's go. See you later, Marie."

As they rode away from the ranchhouse, Waring made a sweeping gesture to the northeast.

"Over there's the open range," he said. "A lot of it—runs way up north."

Slade nodded. "I still think," he said, "that it would be a good notion for you folks to get title to that land; may save you a lot of trouble some time."

"I've been thinking about it ever since we had our talk," Waring admitted. "In fact, I think I will make a try for a section. We have a little spare cash on hand right now, and I reckon there couldn't be a better investment. I'm sure Marie will go along with the notion. Especially if you sort of suggest it," he added with a grin. "She seems to think anything you do must be okay. How about talking to her?"

"I will, if you wish it," Slade agreed.

As they rode, Slade was favorably impressed with the W Diamond. The grass was good, there were plenty of groves and thickets, and sufficient water. Most of the land was level or rolling prairie easy to work.

"A good holding," he summed up. "This has always been excellent country, and always will be, although I've a notion some of it will be turned into farming land in the future."

"I hope not," Waring said. "I hate to see the range spoiled."

"It will be to your advantage in the end," Slade pointed out. "You will be able to purchase fruit and vegetables and grain at a much lower cost. The land down by the bay will be excellent for farming, but not overly good for cows, and there is no sense in adopting a dog-in-the-manger attitude toward it. And meanwhile you might as well reconcile yourself to the inevitable. Farming is coming to Texas, and there is no stopping it. That's one reason why I advised you to get title to that state land if you really wish to hold it, before somebody beats you to the draw."

"Sounds like good advice, and if Marie is agreeable, I'm

prepared to act on it," Waring said. "Much obliged for the tip."

When they returned to the ranchhouse, in the late evening, they received some disquieting news. Al Hodson was waiting for them, bursting with excitement.

"Boss!" he called, as soon as Waring was within earshot, "there's sheep on the range over to the east, a thundering big flock, with half a dozen salty looking hellions herding them. I started to ride to the flock, but they waved me around. I figured the next thing to wave wouldn't be a hat but a rifle barrel, so I headed for home."

17

WARING FAIRLY exploded with anger.

"So the blankety-blank did it!" he bawled. "I'll get the boys together and ride over there and clean out that nest of snakes!"

"Hold it!" Slade said. "You'll do nothing of the kind; you'll stay right here. If you tried that, you'd be in the wrong from the start and Parr would have the law on his side."

"Don't take up for the blankety-blank!" Waring shouted. "You—" His voice trailed off, for the look in Slade's cold eyes boring into his struck him to silence.

"I'm not taking up for him, and I'm not taking up for you," Slade told him. "I am taking up for law and order and the integrity of the state of Texas. By your own admission, that is open range over there, state land, and Parr has as much right, under the law, to run sheep onto it as the cattlemen have to run cows. Do what you threatened to do, and the law as embodied in Sheriff Ross will be against you. You'll be playing right into Parr's hands. You can't bull this thing through, Phil, so don't try it. Besides, if you went sashaying over there looking for trouble, it's very likely that you'd ride into a trap. If Parr has run in sheep, you can rest assured that he has made provisions to keep them in. The chances are you'd just get mowed down by hellions holed up in the brush, and the law would be on their side. You wouldn't have a leg to stand on, if any of you happened to be in a condition to stand at all, which is unlikely. Al only saw half a dozen herders, he said, but you can bet a hatful of pesos that there were more than half a dozen somewhere around. The half-dozen may have been set out as bait. I've a notion that would be Parr's way of doing things. Do you understand, now?"

Under the lash of the Ranger's voice, Waring had cooled considerably.

"Yes, I guess so," he said. "But what the devil are we going to do? If those infernal woollies are allowed to remain, they'll ruin all that range, you can depend on that. Parr won't give a hang, and he won't do anything to prevent it."

"Right now we're doing nothing," Slade replied. "But I think I can guarantee that Parr's sheep won't spoil the range. Right now, sit tight and wait."

"Walt is right, Phil," Marie, who had joined them, broke in. "You listen to him and do what he tells you to do. I'm half-owner, and I'm backing him to the limit."

"All right! All right!" growled Waring. "With the two of you lined up against me, what the devil can I do but knuckle under."

"You won't regret it," she said. "Walt knows what he's about."

"I hope so," Waring replied. "Oh, the devil, let's eat. Getting mad always makes me hungry."

After his third cup of coffee, Waring brightened considerably and achieved a more equable frame of mind.

"Neale Ross says you're never wrong," he observed to Slade. "So I reckon I'm doing the right thing by stringing along with you."

"You certainly are in this instance," Slade agreed. "First thing in the morning I'm riding to town to have a confab with Ross, and to learn what steps he's contemplating to combat possible trouble."

"May I ride with you?" Marie asked quickly.

"Well, you being a cattle spread owner, your presence should tend to enhance my status," he admitted. "Okay with you, Phil?"

"Go ahead," replied Waring. "I'll promise to be good while you're away."

When Slade lay down that night, it was not to sleep for some time. He pondered recent disturbing developments. His problems were multiplying fast. In addition to a murderous outlaw bunch to capture or exterminate, he now had an incipient range war crawling up his pants leg. Swift and strenuous measures were required to prevent that from exploding all over the section. When the word got around, and it wouldn't be long, the cattlemen would be up in arms and a clash between the two factions inevitable if nature were allowed to take its course.

On the surface, Eldon Parr's action appeared to be a deliberate invitation to trouble, but if he read the man aright, and he was convinced he did, Parr would be prepared against trouble. Also, he believed he knew Parr's objective in bringing in the sheep. Well, that objective would not be achieved.

The sheep angle must be taken care of, but it was only incidental to the main problem that confronted him.

With Marie accompanying him, Slade set out for town early the following morning. When they pulled up in front of the sheriff's office, Slade drew something from his saddle pouch that glinted in the sunlight. He tucked it under his arm, where it was not conspicuous. Entering, they found Sheriff Ross in his office and in a bad temper.

"Yes, I heard about it," he said without preamble. "The devil's to pay, and no pitch hot! Why in blazes did Parr do it? He must have known he was going to stir up trouble."

"Neale," Slade said, "did you ever hear of a red herring?"

"A red herring!"

"Yes. A red herring has a very strong and pungent odor, an odor that for some reason known to themselves is very attractive to dogs. A pack will carry the trail of a red herring breast-high without a fault for hours.

"And in the course of rival deer hunts, an unscrupulous contender would drag a red herring across the trail of a deer. The dogs would leave the deer scent and follow the trail of the herring. Finally got to be a saying applied to any distracting practice—'trail of a red herring.'

"And that," he concluded impressively, "is the explanation of the bringing in of sheep by Eldon Parr. He knew well it would kick up a grand hullabaloo, and people in general would for the time being pay little attention to anything else. Which would include yourself. With sheep troubles on your hands, you'd have little time to devote toward the apprehension of the outlaw bunch that masqueraded as men of steel to frighten the superstitious herders and *peons* and therefore simplify their wide-looping operations. Begin to understand?"

"Why—why, in a way," the bewildered peace officer replied. "But why should Parr want to do something that would work to the advantage of an outlaw bunch?"

"Because," Slade replied, "Eldon Parr is the leader of the men of steel."

Marie gasped. Ross nearly jumped out of his chair.

"Walt, have you gone plumb loco?" he sputtered.

"No," Slade answered. "I mean just what I said, and when the proper time comes I'll prove it to your satisfaction and that of everybody else. Straighten this out and take a good look at it."

As he spoke, he laid a folded sheet of metal on the sheriff's desk.

Muttering under his breath, Ross did straighten it out, smoothing the creases.

"Why, it's one of those blasted tin shirts!" he exclaimed.

"Right," Slade nodded. "Now look at the lettering down in the left-hand corner."

With puckered brows, Ross leaned close. H—A—S—J—no, K—I—" he hesitated. "Yes, that's it, Haski." He glanced up expectantly.

"When we looked over the packing plant yesterday" Slade said, "you'll recall we watched some workmen solder rolled sheets of tin to make cans. Well, I got a close look at one of those sheets. Not only was the metal identical with this, but in one corner was the name of the fabricator—'Haskins Mills.' That was where a bad slip was made when the 'suits of armor' for the men of steel were fashioned. It's quite logical to believe that the tin shirts, as you call them, were made in Parr's packing plant. Don't you think so?"

"Why—why, I'll be hanged if it don't look that way," Ross admitted.

"Of course, it's not proof positive that Parr had anything to do with the manufacturing of the phony armor," Slade added. "If questioned, he could say that it was done by somebody in the plant without his knowledge, and without some corroborating evidence, it would be hard to contradict him and make it stick. So let's see what else we've got.

"First, remember the slug Al Hodson stopped on the trail the other day, the slug that was undoubtedly meant for me? Well, aside from you and Doc Price, Eldon Parr was the only person who knew I planned to take that ride. But somebody had a dry-gulcher planted up on the ridge all set to mow me down when I rode past.

"Next. Somebody started a whispering campaign against Phil Waring, insinuating that he was the leader of the outlaw bunch, the men of steel. Another case of a red herring. For Phil is about as capable of originating such a fantastic scheme to play on the superstition of the herders as he is to fly to the moon. Once more, it's logical to think Parr started the whispers. So we come to the wide-looped sheep.

"Those stolen sheep were loaded onto a ship and brought to Parr's packing plant, supposedly from a sheep ranch Parr owns somewhere over east. How? I am positive that I know how it was done, and I plan to put it to the test very soon. And only a man with a more than superficial knowledge of tides and currents and geological formations could have figured that one out. And if there is anyone else in the section who fits into that category, I certainly haven't contacted him."

"Darned if you ain't making out a case against the hellion," growled Ross. "What else?"

"One little thing in particular," Slade replied. "Really a very small thing, but with everything else considered, significant. You'll recall telling me that Parr claimed to have been born and brought up in east Texas. Well, the other night he used a word that no true Texan would be likely to use."

"And that was—" prompted Ross.

" 'Deestrict,' " Slade answered. "A Texan says 'section,' or if for some reason or other he happens to say district, that's how he will pronounce the word—*district* not *deestrict*. The pronunciation *deestrict* is strictly Down East colloquialism. So I was at once convinced that Parr originated someplace other than Texas. And if a man endeavors to cover up his place of origin, he'll bear watching, or so has been my experience."

"I'll throw that ornery toad in the calaboose!" the sheriff raved.

"You'll do nothing of the sort," Slade differed. "Right now there is not an iota of proof against Eldon Parr that would stand up in court. I am confident, in my own mind, that Parr is the man we're after, but being confident about something and proving it to twelve gentlemen in a jury box are horses of a different color. There is no doubt in my mind but that Parr wrecked that ship, the "Compostella," murdered her crew and stole whatever of value was in the captain's safe, but I couldn't prove it—yet. I'll need a little more time to make it possible for you to drop your loop. And that's got me bothered, I'll admit. If the hellion is allowed to run loose, it won't be long before somebody else is murdered."

"What are we going to do?" the sheriff asked helplessly.

"First, we're going to try to prevent a range war between sheep-and cowmen," Slade replied. "Parr's other activities must wait for a while. Get your horse, we're going to pay a visit to the cowmen of the section. Perhaps between the three of us we can cool them down a bit and persuade them not to start a ruckus right off."

Ross hurried out to throw the rig on his mount. Marie turned to Slade.

"Walt," she said, "why are you so intensely interested in this business? Do you, as Felipe, the cook, maintains, 'just go about doing good?' "

"Not exactly, I fear," he replied. "Well, I guess you have a right to know; but it must be strictly a secret between us."

"Another one?" she questioned, with a smile. "Well, I'm used to it."

He drew something from a cunningly concealed secret pocket in his broad leather belt and handed it to her. She gazed at the famous silver star set on a silver circle—the feared and honored badge of the Texas Rangers.

"I suppose I should have guessed it," she said slowly. "You are just what I've always heard a Ranger is. Well, just so you don't range too far. I'm not very hopeful, however," she added.

Outside sounded the sheriff's shout. Slade slipped the badge back into its hiding place, and they joined Ross at the hitchrack.

All day long they rode from ranchhouse to ranchhouse. The section was thoroughly aroused, and threats were voiced. But Sheriff Ross declared flatly that he wouldn't stand for an unprovoked attack on the sheepmen, while Slade used all his powers of persuasion in an endeavor to induce the cowmen to view the matter with equanimity. He felt that Marie's presence and support had a moderating effect.

Ultimately, from each was extracted a reluctant promise not to resort to violence unless the herders first committed some overt act.

It was a promise, however, that was usually tempered with, "But I can't guarantee the boys won't get out of hand if the blasted critters stray onto our range."

As they rode back to town, under the stars, Slade remarked, "Well, we've done the best we can. I believe we did cool them down a bit, but it won't last. I've got to rustle my hocks and bring this thing to a head."

"What do you plan to do?" Ross asked.

"Think it over, for the present," Slade replied evasively. He was "thinking it over," very seriously, planning and reviewing his next move. He did not see fit to confide in his companions because he felt the chore he had in mind could be performed better alone.

They reached town rather tired and very hungry, for they'd had nothing to eat since a cup of coffee and a snack at a ranchhouse around noon.

"We'll put up the broncs and then head for the Post Hole," said Ross. "I'm about ready to topple over."

They proceeded to do just that. Frog-lip Fogarty greeted them warmly.

"Cat's fine," he replied in answer to Slade's question. "Getting better all the time; scratched the cook again because he was slow handing out the liver. We've named him Eat 'Em Up."

They had just finished a very bountiful repast when Eldon Parr entered. Ignoring the hostile glances cast in his direction, he approached the table. Sheriff Ross regarded him with decided disfavor.

"So you did it!" he growled.

"I am within my legal rights in running sheep onto open range," Parr replied coldly. "Is that not so, Mr. Slade?"

"You are within your legal rights," the Ranger conceded.

"And, Sheriff," Parr continued meaningly, "I expect my men to enjoy the protection of the law."

"They'll get it, so long as they stay within the law," Ross answered.

"Thank you," Parr said, and walked out.

"The nervy sidewinder!" Ross snorted. "I believe he'd mosey into a den of grizzlies if he took a notion."

"Yes, a cold proposition," Slade agreed. "I notice he was wearing a coat tonight," he remarked with apparent irrelevance.

"Meaning?"

"Also noticed that there was a slight bulge under the left shoulder," Slade added.

"A shoulder holster man, eh?" commented the sheriff. "It's a fast draw, for a man who knows how to use it."

"And I've a notion Parr knows how to use it, despite his protestations that he is not adept in the use of a gun," Slade said.

"I wouldn't be surprised at anything where he's concerned," grunted Ross. "Well, let's have another drink. How about you, Marie?"

"I'll take some more coffee, if you don't mind," the girl replied.

"Goes for me, too," Slade said.

"Oh, all right, I'll string along with you," the sheriff surrendered. "I hope it don't keep me awake."

"Nothing will keep me awake tonight," Slade answered. "It's been an exhausting day."

Marie smiled.

18

Three hours before dawn, Slade slipped quietly from his room and descended to the hotel lobby. The old night clerk drowsed at his desk. Slade passed without causing him to raise his sleepy head. He made his way to the stable which housed Shadow, opened the door with the key the owner had given him, got the rig on the big black and led him forth, closing and locking the door behind him.

The streets were deserted; there was no sign of activity of any sort. The waves on the beach sounded loud in the great stillness. Here and there a night light glowed dimly. Otherwise, the town was a ghost town, devoid of inhabitants to all appearances. For Port Lavaca slept. Shadow's hoofs clicked softly as Slade turned his nose north by slightly west. Once out on the prairie, he quickened his pace and rode steadily. He was all set to put the test to the first move of his plan to outwit the wily outlaw leader.

He had gathered from Al Hodson the approximate location of the flock of sheep. He figured he had plenty of time to reconnoiter the terrain before daylight and was confident of what he would find there.

Having carefully thought out the whole matter, he had endeavored to put himself in the outlaw leader's place, to reason as he would reason. He believed he had succeeded.

Finally he spotted the flock, a whitish blur in the starlight, the sheep huddled together in sleep. It was bedded down on the open prairie, not a grove or thicket within a mile. Without hesitation, he rode forward boldly and paused a few yards from the assembled woollies. They raised their heads and grumbled a little, then went back to sleep.

"Just as I figured," he told Shadow, "the flock is not guarded at night. Parr doesn't care what happens to it. If a bunch of punchers get out of hand and ride over and slaughter and scatter the sheep, he won't give a hang. Then his case against the cowmen will be made. Meanwhile, his men will be free to operate at will, with all attention focused on the sheep-cattle row. Very clever! The gent has plenty of wrinkles on his horns."

It was clever, but Parr had made a fatal slip in not fully realizing and taking into account the shrewdness of El Halcón.

The real secret of Walt Slade's outstanding success as a Ranger lay in his uncanny ability to think as the outlaws thought, to anticipate their actions and provide against them. There were plenty of Rangers with fast gunhands, cold nerve and undaunted courage. But Slade not only outshot the owl-hoots, he out-thought them.

He glanced at the stars. "Guess we'd better be moseying, feller," he said. "Come daylight there'll be three or four gents riding around out here, ostensibly keeping a sharp lookout and standing guard over the woollies. You'll notice the flock is placed within sight of anybody riding the north-south trail, and horsemen are frequent on that trail. They see the sheep, they see the herders, and draw their own conclusions. Which is exactly what Parr wants them to do. Okay, we'll see if we can't tangle that smart and salty gent's twine for him. That is, if he doesn't tangle ours. He's no pushover and may well be weaving a snare for us while we think we're setting a trap for him. Well, we'll see."

He turned the horse and rode swiftly south by east, arriving at Port Lavaca an hour after sunrise.

After caring for Shadow, he repaired to the hotel lobby, where he found Marie.

"So! Out prowling again, eh?" she remarked resignedly. "All right, let's go, I waited to eat breakfast with you."

At the Post Hole, a waiter smiled sleepily but served them deftly enough. Eat 'Em Up, the cat, strolled in from the kitchen, rubbed against Slade's leg and purred loudly.

"He remembers you," Marie observed, adding with feminine accuracy, "only he isn't."

"Isn't what?"

"He isn't a he, he's a she. No wonder it fell for you, head over heels."

"Anyhow, she didn't scratch me," he smiled.

"She should have, the way you turned her over to someone else and walked out on her. Well, like all other women, she'll have to learn to take it. How about some more coffee?"

They enjoyed a leisurely breakfast, after which Slade rolled and smoked a cigarette. Pinching out the butt, he said, "Ready to travel? We'll head back to the spread as soon as you are."

The ride to the W Diamond ranchhouse was peaceful, and Slade spent the day loitering around the yard and talking with Waring and those of the hands who were not out on the range. But again the dark before the dawn the following morning found him in the saddle, riding swiftly south by west.

"Well, Shadow, here it comes, the big test, which will prove whether or not my hunch is a straight one. I think it is, but you can never tell for sure about such things. Freakish, all right, but not beyond what is to be expected from a mind like Eldon Parr's. Somehow, I believe, he stumbled onto the formation and realized the use to which it could be put. The fellow's no mean geologist, and I've a notion, too, that he has had considerable to do with the sea. June along, horse, and let's see if we're following a cold trail. Betcha we're not."

Shadow's answering snort seemed to say he didn't approve of gambling in any form and was taking no bets. Slade chuckled and glanced at the eastern sky, which was already flushing a tremulous rose.

The stars grew pale and paler still, dwindled to needle-points of steel piercing the black velvet robe of the night. The rose in the east deepened to scarlet, flamed crimson, shot and spangled with gold. Spear upon spear of glorious light flashed to the zenith, fell earthward like glowing javelins to pierce the shadows, fire and melt the veils of mist. A bird sang a joyous note, and it was day.

Slade rode on through the increasing warmth as the sun climbed higher. It was halfway up the long slant of the eastern sky when he sighted, still dim with distance, the long and low ridge which fronted the coastline of rough water. As he drew nearer, he saw that the northwestern slope was much more rugged, for erosion had denuded the limestone core of the rise. Also, it was cracked and broken and fissured, the effects of frosts and thaws throughout the ages.

Before long he was riding not far from its base, turning Shadow's nose more to the east. And shortly he uttered an exclamation.

Scoring the softer earth were many small prints, the marks left by the sharp chisel-hoofed feet of sheep. There were also some hoofmarks of cattle, and many left by the irons of horses, some of them comparatively recent.

"Told you it was a straight hunch, horse," he exulted. "Here's where they bring the wide-looped stock to load it on the ships. Now all we have to do is find out how they do it."

"Which may prove more of a chore than you think," Shadow appeared to observe complacently. Slade chuckled and rode on, scanning the broken slant of the ridge with meticulous care.

Really, he didn't need to, for the prints were perfect guideposts. On they led, then turned abruptly toward the slope. A moment later the Ranger saw that they led to the mouth of an opening some ten or twelve feet wide by eight or better high which scored the face of a beetling, clifflike formation.

Tense with excitement, he rode up to the opening. Then he turned in the saddle and scanned the prairie. He could see for miles over the level surface. Nowhere was there any sign of life.

"Looks like we've got everything to ourselves," he remarked. "Not wearing a tail."

Nearby was a bristle of thicket. Dismounting, he led Shadow to it where the growth cast a cooling shade. He slipped out the bit, loosened the cinches.

"Now you can take it easy while I investigate that crack," he said. Shadow responded by beginning to crop grass. Slade looked about and spotted a stand of sotol, a very prevalent growth in the section. He broke off a number of dry stalks for torches, lighted one and entered the cave, the floor of which had a sharp downward slope. Holding the torch aloft and keeping close to the side wall, which was studded with knobs and juts of stone and scored by crevices, he strode along cautiously, scanning the floor for obstructions or pitfalls and seeing none.

For several hundred yards he groped his way along the steep descent of the bore. Abruptly the wall to his left, which reflected the torchlight, vanished and was replaced by thick darkness the torchlight could not pierce; the cave had widened greatly. And to his ears came a faint whispering, coming and going, and a draft of salt air bent the sotol flame. Without a doubt, the rocky tunnel led to the sea.

"I was right!" he exclaimed aloud. "But I still don't know how they do it."

He had covered a couple of hundred yards when the rock wall to his left suddenly resumed, and he again found himself in a tunnel some thirty feet in width. He advanced cautiously, peering and listening, until he was something like two hundred yards down the narrowed stone tunnel. Abruptly he realized that the whispering had loudened to a murmur which grew to a mutter, a low rumble. He halted, staring and listening. Then he whirled and ran for his life.

He had covered less than half the distance to where the bore widened when he saw the pale vision of terror that accompanied the sound—the crest of onward rushing water!

19

THE TORCH flickered out, extinguished by a blast of wet air. He hugged the right wall as the water swirled about his ankles, rose to his knees. Frantically he plowed through it, clutching at the knobs and spikes that protruded from the wall, hooking his fingers into crevices. The water frothed about his thighs, his waist, rose breast high. Were it not for the knobs of stone by aid of which he hauled himself along he would have been swept off his feet and destroyed. As it was, he was verging on despair. His strength was ebbing. The torrent was washing his shoulders, flinging spray into his face, choking him, stopping his breath. It was lapping his chin when at last it began to shallow, which it did swiftly. He hurled himself forward, sloshed through a final film, staggered onward a few steps and sank to the rocky floor, utterly exhausted, his breath coming in hoarse gasps, his heart pounding like an overburdened engine.

For minutes he lay prone. "This won't do," he muttered as he revived a little. His teeth were chattering with cold, his body aching from the terrific pounding of the water. Summoning all his strength, he floundered to his feet and staggered up the steep incline. After what seemed an eternity of painful effort he reached the open air. Shadow gave an inquiring snort as he sat down on the grass, removed his boots and emptied them of water. He waved reassuringly to the horse and stretched out in the warm sunshine. At once his drenched clothing began to steam, the chill that seemed in his very bones to evaporate.

For quite a while he lay motionless, then, his strength returning, he sat up, fumbled his papers and tobacco from their waterproof pouch, shook a dry match from a tightly corked flat bottle—the cowboy's waterproof matchbox—and rolled and lighted a cigarette. He smoked it slowly, in deep drags, pinched out the butt and tossed it aside.

"Well, I was right in every detail," he told Shadow. "Made one little slip, though, that very nearly caused me to get my comeuppance. I shouldn't have made it, either, after seeing how that inshore current rushes into the east cave mouth. Really inexcusable for me not to realize what that meant."

Shadow cocked an attentive ear. Slade continued:

"What I carelessly overlooked is the fact that from the outer east cave mouth, the slope is steeply downward. As a result, a head of water accumulates at the bottom of the slope before the trend reverses to a much more gentle upward slope in this direction. When the tide rises, and it rises very swiftly on that shore, the accelerated current shoves the head of water up the gentle slope, precipitately, so that it rushes across the widened cave and boils into the downward sloping tunnel which ends in the west opening at the bay's edge. Just a simple example of hydraulics. Understand?" Shadow snorted and reached for a mouthful of grass.

"Well," Slade added, "I'm feeling pretty good again and somewhat dried out, so I'm going to have another peek into that hole. This time I think I'll find what I'm looking for."

Securing more torches, he re-entered the cave. When he reached the point where it widened, he turned sharply to the left and a moment later saw what he was searching for.

Close to the end wall of the widened cave were three large, roughly constructed flatboats or lighters. They were set on rollers made of carefully trimmed tree trunks, and each was fully a dozen feet wide and more than twenty-five long.

"And they'll pack a lot of woollies, or quite a few cows," Slade told himself.

Now the modus operandi of the wide-loopers was perfectly plain. When the tide reached flood stage and began to ebb, the boats would be shoved into the water and the gentle current would take them through the west cave and well out to sea, where a ship would be waiting to receive their cargo. Then the in-shore current, running swiftly and directly through its deep channel scoured out between the ledges in the course of the ages, would return them to the cave, where they would be caught and moored. The ship would proceed with the sheep and unload them at Eldon Paar's packing plant.

Yes, very simple, but the hellion who conceived the scheme and put it into operation was a crooked genius if there ever was one, Slade told himself. Why the devil couldn't such ingenuity be directed into legitimate channels! It was a question that more than once had plagued the Ranger when he had uncovered the amazingly clever but devious manipulations of one who had somehow taken the wrong fork of the trail.

Of course the stakes in this particular instance were large. Every stolen flock represented thousands of dollars, clear profit for Parr and his associates. The same applied to the improved cows of the section, for which there were plenty of ready markets.

Greed! The root of much evil.

With a last look around, Slade returned to Shadow. Not far inside the cave mouth he saw evidence that horses had frequently occupied a space near the wall, evidently left there by the rustlers when they entered the tunnel.

"All set to drop our loop, horse," he told the black. "Well, I noticed a little creek a couple of miles on the back trail. We'll stop off there, and I'll cook something to eat and you can have a good drink. We're in no particular hurry, and I'm hungry. Pity I'm not a grass burner like you—would save a lot of work and lost time. But an ordinary mortal like myself can't live on grass, like Nebuchadnezzar. That requires a special dispensation of Providence and peculiar digestive organs. Let's go!"

Slade let Shadow take his time on the return trip, and it was late when he reached the W Diamond ranchhouse. When he entered the living room he found Marie waiting up for him.

"You're a sight!" she exclaimed. "What have you been doing, swimming with your clothes on? Never mind, now. I imagine you're starved, and I've kept something warm for you and plenty of hot coffee. Do you want to change before you eat?"

"I have a clean shirt and overalls in my pouch that should feel better than this wrinkled mess," he admitted.

"Go ahead, I'll have everything ready when you come down."

As he ate, Slade recounted his experiences in the cave. She listened in silence until he finished, then, "I suppose you plan to set a trap for those men."

"Naturally," he replied. "I feel pretty sure they may try something the first stormy night. They haven't had much luck with their ventures of late, and an outlaw leader has to keep the money coming in if he hopes to hold his men in line; I don't think Parr likes to part with any of his own. Tomorrow I'll ride down and have a little talk with Lopez and Garcia and the other flock owners; perhaps we can arrange something."

"Tomorrow, we will ride," she corrected.

"All right," he agreed. "I don't see any reason for getting

into a ruckus this trip. We'll cut across the prairie and bypass the town."

They rode together the following morning. It was a long ride but a pleasant one. A hearty welcome was accorded them at all the *haciendas* visited. Lopez, Garcia and Telo agreed to go along with Slade's plan and were confident they could swing the other owners into line.

"We're all glad to lend a hand in an effort to get rid of those pests," said Lopez. "I believe what you've figured out will work. Sure worth giving it a whirl, anyhow."

"Yes, I believe it will work," Slade agreed. "I'm pretty sure they're keeping a watch on your holdings, and when they see the flocks are unguarded they will be tempted to make a try for one. They figure, I think, that the recent setbacks they have suffered will lull the flock owners into a false sense of security; that's the way the outlaw mind works. In my opinion, the first stormy night they'll make a move. Anyhow, I can't see that anything will be lost, and if it doesn't work, we'll have to try something else."

"How does the ship know when a flock is coming out to be loaded?" Lopez wondered.

"They are constantly in touch with one," Slade replied. "The captain will know approximately when to expect cargo and will stand off-shore waiting. They'll signal him with a fire, a fire that would lure another vessel to its doom, as in the case of the "Compostella." No trouble to charter a ship for such a chore. Smuggling is rampant all the way from here to Port Isabel, and unscrupulous skippers are not averse to making a dishonest dollar in any manner that presents itself. Parr has contacts and puts them to use. Well, now all we can do is wait and see if they'll come to our lure. Keep an eye on the weather and be ready to move at the first sign of a bad night."

A tedious wait followed. Although it was the season of Gulf storms, day after day of fine weather prevailed. The salvage crew arrived, and the "Compostella" was pried loose from the reefs and patched up sufficiently to limp to port. The agents at Galveston repeated their disavowal of any explanation as to why she had been in Matagorda Bay.

"If they know, they sure ain't talking," Sheriff Ross told Slade. "I've a notion they're telling the truth. Those Gulf skippers in coastwise trade are a tricky lot and pull things the owners don't know about."

Eldon Parr's sheep continued to graze on the open range

land, and the cattlemen, sticking to their promise, ignored them.

"I've a notion Parr's beginning to feel that he sort of missed fire, as it were," Slade chuckled to Ross. "I expect he's in quite an irritable mood. I hope so, for if he really loses his temper, his judgment will go by the board."

"Uh-huh, you mentioned that the night he had the run-in with Al Hodson," Ross replied. "I believe you're right."

And then one evening clouds began banking up in the southeast. By morning the sky was overcast and a damp wind was blowing in from the bay.

Slade had a good look at the weather and said, "If they really intend to make a try, I think this is it. Looks like a real storm will be booming in by nightfall. Made to order for them. They can hole up the critters in the cave if the weather is too stormy and wait until it quiets down a bit before shoving them out to the ship. Yes, this should be it."

In the late evening, Miguel Lopez, Garcia and Telo arrived at the W Diamond ranchhouse, the decided gathering point. Sebastian Hernandez, Lopez' range boss, accompanied his *patrón*. As darkness fell, Sheriff Ross and his three dupties showed up, one at a time. The W Diamond punchers, who were rarin' to go, completed the posse.

"Parr hasn't been seen for two days," the sheriff announced. "The boys have been keeping a lookout, and they haven't spotted hair nor hide of him."

"That's encouraging," Slade commented. "Evidently he's out rounding up his bunch and preparing to direct operations. I was afraid he might keep in the clear and perhaps give us the slip. It would be like him to have a getaway plan—he's a crafty devil. Well, I guess we'd better start—we've got a long ride ahead of us, and I figure that if they do try something tonight, they'll be shoving the flock to the cave somewhere around the dark hour before daylight, which will be late with the sky overcast the way it is."

"Wind's getting stronger by the minute," Lopez observed. "It's going to be a wild night."

"In more ways than one, the chance are," Slade said. "So long, Marie, be seeing you."

Ten minutes later the posse was riding south by west through a night of wind and rain and darkness.

They rode at a steady pace, with little conversation. Al Hodson carried a bulky bundle across the pommel of his saddle, a quantity of oil-soaked cotton waste wrapped in a waterproof poncho. Others packed a couple of lanterns that Slade thought might prove useful.

Midnight came and went; an hour passed, and another. The wind still blew, but the rain had ceased and the cloud wrack was thinning. Now large objects could be dimly seen.

"All to the good," Slade said, apropos of the weather. "Now we'll be able to see them approach. With the wind and the rain like they were a while ago, we'd have had to largely depend on guesswork."

With unerring accuracy he led the way to the limestone ridge. Finally it loomed darkly against the southern sky, where an occasional star peeped through the clouds. He turned slightly to the east.

"Over there is an overhang with a hollow in the cliff that's almost a shallow cave," he explained. "It will be perfect to hole up the cayuses."

Without difficulty they found the hollow in the rock face. Here they dismounted.

"Bring along the bundle of waste and the lanterns," Slade said in low tones.

One deputy was left to watch the horses and make sure they kept quiet. The rest of the posse, with Slade leading, stole west along the face of the ridge. A dozen paces from the cave mouth, Slade called a halt.

"I'm going ahead and look things over," he whispered. "Don't want to walk into a trap or something. "I want to be sure of the lay of the land. No, I don't want anybody with me; one can go quieter than two."

Hugging the rock wall, he reached the cave mouth, glided into it, pressing against the east wall, careful to make no sound. But as he neared where the cave widened, he halted abruptly. Ahead was a faint, flickering glow. Things weren't working out so well. Without a doubt somebody was in the cave and had a fire going.

After a long moment of hesitation, he resumed his forward creep. He reached the point where the east wall of the tunnel ended, peered cautiously around it.

Just beyond where the boats were drawn against the end wall, above where the water turned as it rushed from the east cave, a fire burned briskly. Standing on the far side of the blaze, warming his back, was a man, his form vaguely seen and distorted by the flames.

20

SLADE HALTED AGAIN. Now what the devil was he to do? He could shoot the fellow, but that would be in the nature of a cold-blooded killing, beyond the pale for a Ranger. Besides, he earnestly desired to take him alive if possible. From him, he might glean some valuable information.

Cover him and order him to elevate? Too risky, under the circumstances. He could barely make out his form from where he stood. With one leap the hellion would be in darkness, the advantage all on his side. Slade knew he couldn't tell whether he was raising his hands as ordered or going for his gun. He had to get to where he could see around the fire, which also was unpleasantly risky.

Gambling that the fellow would not turn, he stole forward, brushing against the boats, which provided a little shadow from the reflection of the fire on the rock wall. Half a dozen paces he covered, three more, another three. Now he was opposite the edge of the fire and only a couple of yards from where the outlaw lounged, absorbing the comforting warmth. And the unexpected happened. As Slade took one more stride, reaching for his gun, his foot came down on a dry and crooked branch that had rolled from a nearby heap. It broke with a crack like a gunshot in the stillness.

The man whirled, reaching for his gun. Slade leaped at the same instant. He caught the descending wrist, pinned it against the other's side. They grappled fiercely, half in the fire, half out, scattering glowing embers in every direction.

With a yell, the outlaw threw a blow with his free hand. His whizzing fist grazed the Ranger's jaw. Then Slade's right hand shot out in turn, landed solidly. The fellow gasped, sagging. Slade struck again, and his fist thudded against the side of the other's head. He went limp and fell, his wrist jerking out of El Halcón's grasp.

But even as he hit the ground, Slade was on top of him, plucking the gun from his holster. He cast it aside, straightened up, poised for instant action. However, the fellow was still dazed by the Ranger's blows. He mumbled, groaned, his limbs flopped.

Satisfied that there was no further threat from him, Slade waited a few minutes until he had somewhat collected his scattered faculties. Then he thrust his hands under his shoulders and jerked him to a sitting position to the accompaniment of gabbled oaths.

"All right," he said, "seeing as you're able to swear so well, try standing up. Up, I said!"

The prod of a gun muzzle in the ribs emphasized the command. The fellow lurched erect and stood weaving, still a bit groggy. Slade waited until he was firm on his feet.

"All right, head for the outside," he ordered. "Careful, now, I've got an itchy trigger finger."

Still mumbling curses, the captive obeyed. With Slade's gun muzzle against his back, he weaved and stumbled up the slant of the cave to the outer air.

"What in blazes!" Sheriff Ross sputtered as they emerged from the cave. "Did you grab 'em all by yourself?"

"Nope, just this one," Slade replied.

"Fine!" exclaimed Al Hodson. "Let's hang him right now—no sense in waiting."

"We'll give him a chance to talk, first," Slade said. "Light one of the lanterns."

"A-a-aw!" said Hodson, in disappointed tones.

The lantern was lighted. Slade regarded the prisoner. He was a husky, hard-looking individual, his eyes sparkling with resentment.

"Your bunch is grabbing off a flock tonight?" Slade asked.

The prisoner scowled and remained sullenly silent.

"All right, Al, get your rope," Slade said.

"Whe-e-e!" chortled Hodson. "I just love a necktie party." He turned to go.

"Wait, wait," yammered the captive. "I'll talk!"

"All right, talk," Slade said. "Answer my question."

"Yes, they figure to run a bunch of Telo's woollies that ain't got anybody watching them."

Slade nodded. Telo swore.

"And why were you left here? What are you supposed to do?" Slade asked.

The outlaw hesitated. Looking cheerful, Hodson again turned to go.

"All right, keep that big hellion off me and I'll come clean," the rustler said. "When I hear the woollies coming I'm supposed to wave a lantern to let the boys know everything is okay."

"One more question," Slade said. "Is Eldon Parr with the bunch tonight?" The prisoner nodded.

"Take him over with the horses, tie him up and gag him," Slade directed. "The rest of you come along with me. Here, Al, hang onto this lantern. Stay here, and if you see or hear anything, wave it. Then hightail down the cave. I'll be back as soon as I get the boys set. Somebody light that other lantern, and don't forget the bundle of waste."

As they proceeded down the bore, Slade jerked his thumb to the left.

"Over there is where they leave the horses, but they drive the sheep on to the big cave," he said.

When they reached the main cave, Slade deployed his men with care—in the darkness beyond the fire and a little distance down the cave, making sure they knew their positions.

"You don't have to stay there, but be all set to dive back when I come with the word," he directed. "And keep the fire going. That way, their eyes will be dazzled by it. Plenty of wood stacked over there. A branch that slid from the heap nearly caused me to get my comeuppance. All right, everything understood? I'm going back to keep Al company."

When he reached the outside, he found Hodson leaning against the rock, smoking a cigarette.

"Everything quiet out here," he said. "Now what?"

"Now there's nothing to do but wait," Slade replied.

It proved to be a long and tedious wait, and Slade began to grow anxious. Perhaps something had miscarried. Perhaps the canny Parr had smelled a mouse and abandoned the try for one of the flocks. It was with relief that he finally heard, thin with distance, the bleating of the tired and disgusted sheep. A few minutes later his keen eyes spotted the crawling whitish mass that was the advancing woollies. He waited a few minutes more, then waved the lantern.

A moment later an answering light swayed and bobbed in the distance. He waved the lantern again.

"Let's go," he told his companion. They hurried down the bore.

The men of the posse were lounging about the fire when they reached the main cave, smoking and talking.

"Get set," Slade told them. "They should be here in another twenty minutes. Neale, you are the peace officer and in charge; you do the talking. Perhaps they'll surrender, but I doubt it—they're salty. You have to give them the chance, but if they don't take it, shoot fast and shoot straight. Okay, everything understood?"

He gathered up the unrolled bundle of oily waste and stood ready to toss it on the fire.

Another tedious wait followed. Then, abruptly, the bleating of the sheep filled the cave. A few more minutes and, complaining querulously, they streamed into the range of the firelight, a goodly number. Following them came eight or nine men, shoving them along.

Slade waited another moment, then with an underhand pitch he tossed the waste onto the fire.

With a roar, a sheet of flame shot up to the rock roof, making the scene bright as day, revealing the rigid forms of the astounded outlaws, Eldon Parr looming in the rear. Sheriff Ross's voice rang out.

"Elevate! You're covered. In the name of the law!"

"Caught settin'," as it were, it looked like the bunch would be taken without the firing of a shot. Then Eldon Parr's right hand streaked to his left armpit. Instantly the air rocked and quivered to the thunder of the guns.

Unprepared, dazed, the outlaws never had a chance. Half their number went down under that first bellowing volley. Slade shot with both hands, and two more fell. The two remaining on their feet flung down their weapons and howled for mercy.

Slade saw Eldon Parr whirl and dash madly across the cave. He swerved to the left and raced down the steep incline. Slade bounded after him, Ross and Miguel Lopez pounding along in his rear.

They reached the point where the west cave narrowed, sped on. Slade could hear the beat of Parr's boots well to the front. He raised his gun to risk a shot.

Then he heard something else—the low, ominous mutter he had heard once before. He spun about and once more ran for his life.

"Back!" he shouted to Ross and Lopez. "Back! Run! Run!"

The order was obeyed without question, but the surging water was above their knees when they panted up the slope of the main cave to safety.

"Blazes! What an infernal hole this is!" gasped Ross, swabbing at the sweat which streamed down his face. "I never want to see it again. Never heard of the like."

"There's a somewhat similar formation on the coast of Borneo," Slade observed. "It's called the Blue Grotto, somewhat resembling the famous one on the Island of Capri, but dangerous, whereas the one on Capri is safe. Water does funny things to a limestone formation. Chances are the whole thing will fall in some day and be blocked. Incidentally, this entire coastline is changing rapidly, due to tides and the filling up of the channel. Fifty years from now, persons living today wouldn't recognize it if they happened to be still alive and riding this way. Quite likely the trail will be gone, and where there is now grassland will be marshes and bayous. Tides are fierce in the bay, although they will become gentler as the channel fills, and are eating away the coast rapidly. Well, it looks like Señor Parr has wide-looped his last bunch of sheep. He's taking a long, long trip."

"I wonder why he did it?" remarked Lopez. "He must have known the danger."

"Perhaps he got confused and turned the wrong way," Slade hazarded. "Then again he may have figured he could reach the sea mouth and swim with that smooth off-shore current to the waiting ship. A strong swimmer could likely do it. Well, it doesn't matter, so long as he and his hell-raising are finished. Let's go see how the boys made out with the prisoners. I want to talk to them."

They found everything under control, six of the outlaws dead. Slade questioned the two prisoners, who were voluble enough.

With the bodies of the slain outlaws roped to their horses and the three captives closely guarded, they headed for town.

"Everything about as I figured," Slade told Sheriff Ross as they rode together, a little to the rear. "Parr heard about that peculiar cave formation and the resulting currents from an old prospector. He figured how he could put it to use, just as he figured he could play on the superstitious fears of the herders with his men of steel masquerade. So he set up in business in Port Lavaca and had a good thing going. He stole that flock of sheep from a ranch over to the east and ran it on the open range to, as I thought, distract attention from his other activities, for things were getting a mite hot for him."

"After the arrival of El Halcón," the sheriff put in. Slade smiled.

"I got the name of the ship that transported the stolen woollies and cows," Slade resumed. "She's the "Isabella" out of Nautla, Mexico. You can notify the Customs people, and they'll run her down. The cows were sold in Mexico, the sheep run to Parr's packing plant, of course. The wrecked ship, the

"Compostella," was coming back after a run to Mexico with contraband goods. The unscrupulous hellion heard of it and lured her onto the rocks and grabbed off the money in the safe after murdering the captain and the crew. He planned other wrecking ventures, the prisoners told me. They'll tie up any loose ends for you in hope of saving their own necks. So I guess that about completes the chore."

"And what do you plan to do now?" Ross asked.

"I'm riding north," Slade answered. "Captain Jim will have another chore lined up for me by the time I get back to the post; I've taken overly long on this one."

With the led horses, progress was rather slow, and it was noon when they rode into Port Lavaca, where astounded citizens listened to the story they had to tell and showered Slade and the sheriff with praise.

The horses were cared for, the prisoners locked up. Then everybody trooped into the Post Hole for a hefty surrounding, after which Ross and his deputies went to bed. Waring and his hands decided they weren't too tired and that a mite of celebration was in order. Lopez and the other flock owners elected to join them.

After he was sure Shadow was sufficiently rested, Slade got the rig on and led him from the stable and to the rack in front of the Post Hole. He called Waring out and drew him aside.

"Tell Marie for me that I'll be seeing her soon, I hope," he said.

"But, blast it! I'd hoped you'd stay here and sign on with me," the disappointed rancher complained.

"Not just yet," Slade said, swinging into the saddle. He gestured to the north, where in the far distance a tall hill glowed golden in the low-lying sun.

"Phil, there's something calling from the other side of that top," he said smilingly as he spoke to Shadow and gathered up the reins.

He did not see fit to explain it was the voice of duty that called.

www.ingramcontent.com/pod-product-compliance
Lightning Source LLC
Chambersburg PA
CBHW020657180626
46816CB00003B/1321